THE AWAKENING OF THE SELF

TALES OF A
SHAMAN
IN THE MAKING

KATIE MCLAUGHLIN

BALBOA.
PRESS
A DIVISION OF HAY HOUSE

Balboa Press books may be ordered through booksellers or by contacting:

Balboa Press
A Division of Hay House
1663 Liberty Drive
Bloomington, IN 47403
www.balboapress.com
1 (877) 407-4847

Because of the dynamic nature of the Internet, any web addresses or
links contained in this book may have changed since publication and
may no longer be valid. The views expressed in this work are solely those
of the author and do not necessarily reflect the views of the publisher,
and the publisher hereby disclaims any responsibility for them.

The author of this book does not dispense medical advice or prescribe
the use of any technique as a form of treatment for physical, emotional,
or medical problems without the advice of a physician, either directly
or indirectly. The intent of the author is only to offer information
of a general nature to help you in your quest for emotional and
spiritual well-being. In the event you use any of the information in
this book for yourself, which is your constitutional right, the author
and the publisher assume no responsibility for your actions.

Any people depicted in stock imagery provided by Thinkstock are
models, and such images are being used for illustrative purposes only.
Certain stock imagery © Thinkstock.

Print information available on the last page.

ISBN: 978-1-5043-8088-1 (sc)
ISBN: 978-1-5043-8089-8 (hc)
ISBN: 978-1-5043-8090-4 (e)

Library of Congress Control Number: 2017908101

Balboa Press rev. date: 06/13/2017

CONTENTS

I dedicate this book to you, especially to that part of you that longs for something sacred. I dedicate this book to your soul—the part of you that is divine and eternal, the part of you that knows you came here with a powerful mission. I dedicate this book to the part of you that is mesmerized by the beauty of this planet, the mind-blowing effect of a good song on your body, the delight of a rainy afternoon, the scent of coffee, and the permanent search for awakening.

I dedicate this book to that part of you because that's the part of you that will enjoy this book the most. This book is mystery with a spark of divinity; it is alchemy of past pain; it is lessons you can carry in your pocket through every walk of life. This book is messy and imperfectly beautiful, just like we should all be.

This book aims to serve you and help you observe, through my personal experience, a whole new world of possibility. This book aims to not only help you believe in the impossible, but understand that the "impossible" is our true nature.

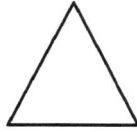

A MESSAGE FOR YOU

You are exactly where you need to be. The struggles you face now, you will be giving others advice about. You are strong. Not the regular kind of strong; you are *strong* because behind you there's an army of light. The whole Universe stands behind you. You are on a mission, and nothing can stop you. Your dreams are yours to take. You are guided. You are provided for. You are doing it. You are already doing it.

Katie McLaughlin

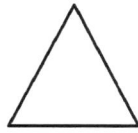

△

PREFACE

Writing is a form of healing for me. Then I don't succeed right away at healing what is bothering me through meditation and energy work, I feel inclined to write about it. This helps me put everything into perspective and understand deeper truths behind what is happening at the moment. This book's writing process began and was left suspended till a later date several times, as the story continued to unfold in my life. I knew as soon as I started my Shamanic Training that I needed to record all those experiences in order to remember them all clearly, and I did, but then I'd stop because I felt like something was missing. The file lingered in my computer for months, and every time I'd see it, I felt like I should probably be writing and finishing it. Then life began to unfold, showing me how I needed to be patient because the book first needed to happen in my life and then on a page. So, I waited and observed how all the pieces fell together accordingly, at last bringing this book into existence.

Tales of a Shaman in the Making is a fiction novel, yet it's inspired by my own story. Few details have been changed to help the reader have the best experience possible reading this book. All names of characters and personalities have been altered for the same reasons. Every vision, journey, and spiritual happening described in this book was real. I want the reader to know, however, that even though my experience was very dramatic, back then, it never lacked beauty.

If you feel inclined to begin walking on the shaman's path, please do, as you will discover your experience will be tailored to your own needs, as mine was. Looking back and rereading this work, I can observe how much in me has healed. I see shamanism with a completely different set of eyes now. I see it only as light and love, leaving out of it all the fear-based perspectives I used to have while going through the experiences described in the book. Through the years, I have seen my own vibration shift and a more elevated perspective become engrained within me. Nevertheless, I believe we need to honor every step of the process and be completely vulnerable and honest about where we have been before reaching a state of comfort. I love reading about my old, scared, clueless self, as I know the road of improvement is a lifelong journey.

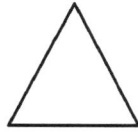

ACKNOWLEDGMENTS

First and foremost, I'd like to express my gratitude to the Universe for placing these experiences in my life and my spirit guides who encouraged me, guided me, and directed my efforts for this work to be the best it can be at this time. I'd like to thank my teacher who gifted me with these years of self-discovery, healing, and profound transformation. My life wouldn't be what it is today if it wasn't for you. Thank you.

I'd like to thank my mother, for giving me her entire life unconditionally, without complaints or reservations. Mom, I couldn't possibly ask for a better mom. Every effort you've done on our behalf, every hour of work, every tear shed, every bit of advice you've given me, every hug, every disagreement, I cherish them all—everything, all of it. Thank you for absolutely every interaction we've ever had. I love you and will forever. I'm grateful to you in ways I don't know how to express. Thank you for allowing me to be; thank you for loving me for who I truly am.

I'd like to thank my sister for continuously supporting me, listening to me incessantly, and being the one and only person I can share everything with, no matter how crazy. Thank you for coming back; thank you for all the lessons shared and for being proof of how miracles exist. Thank you for your kindness.

I'd like to thank my family for their presence in my life, their love, the infinite sessions of advice in the kitchen, and how every time I fall they are always there to hold me. Thank you for reminding me how unstoppable I can be, if I wish to. I'd like to thank my book coach, for holding the space for me so professionally, lovingly, and impeccably and for being my friend and ally in the hilarious and extremely unusual life we live. I'd like to thank my entire tribe, the family I got to choose, the family that chose me—my students. If they only knew how they teach me more every day than I could teach them over a lifetime. Thank you for your trust and helping me see the value of my mission. I love you guys with my entire heart. Thank you for being my first group, a group of warrior souls in the search to make a positive difference in this world. There are no words to describe how proud I will always feel of you all, no matter what.

I'd like to thank my aunt for allowing me to be as I am without judgment. Thank you for being that safe space within the family in which I can shine my light brightly and honestly. Thank you for understanding me and how misunderstood my experiences can be. Thank you for seeing within me the light that will take me everywhere I need to go, not necessarily everywhere I'm expected to. I love you. Thanks to our whole beautiful family for the unconditional support provided through good times and not so good times; I love each one of you deeply.

I'd like to thank everyone at Hay House for the

continuous source of inspiration and guidance. Thanks to everyone who put together the Writer's Workshop. Thanks to Balboa Press and the way they open the road ahead for all of us new authors.

Finally, I'd like to thank every soul I've encountered on my path. Whether it is through yoga, meditations, retreats, bars, travels, flights, social media, etc. You have all contributed to who I am today. Thank you, thank you, thank you.

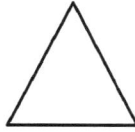

CHAPTER 1

"So, you are saying that just by being here I'm automatically committing to this for the rest of my life?" Amber asked, showing a look of confusion and urgency on her delicate face as she faced the teacher and the rest of the group.

The energy of the space shifted into nervousness as they all faced the teacher, awaiting anxiously for her reply.

"It's not like that," Simone replied and laughed lightheartedly. She could perceive the concern flooding the eyes of the thirteen women gathered in a circle around her.

"Shamanism is the energy medicine of the Americas— the medicine that has healed humans for thousands of years before hospitals and pharmaceuticals even existed. Through the path of shamanism, you will all receive great wisdom. You will remember where your soul came from, what it has gone through, and what your mission is here. You will awaken your psychic powers, intuitive abilities, and connection to the universe around you. As you do that, it will be natural for you to stay in the shamanic path, because it's very likely you'll love it." She spoke politely as she sat cross-legged on the floor near the group altar, which was filled with colorful healing crystals, feathers, and sacred items of all sorts.

"I honestly don't know what I'm getting myself into. I have to admit it makes me really nervous to initiate something I might later regret," Amber shared with the group with complete vulnerability. The trees around the circle danced alongside the afternoon breeze, and the golden glow of a beautiful Panamanian sunset embraced the whole space. The grass was lush, flowers were abundant, and the smoke of sweet-scented incense filled the air.

"I was drawn here with a longing for something— something I can't even explain. I have lived my life with a burning sensation in my heart the whole time. It feels like I'm missing something. I've been waiting for anything or anyone to answer all my questions, waiting to remember something I have forgotten." A few tears began to flow down Amber's cheeks. She immediately dried them with her hands.

The group looked at her compassionately. Her wavy brown hair covered her shoulders and forehead. Her tiny nose was red, and her big green eyes were filled with tears she clearly didn't expect. There was beauty in her pain. There was a sincere sense of truth within her that everyone could acknowledge.

"I think we need more information about this, Simone. It seems like we are completely unaware of what the commitment is for this journey," Silvia, one of the thirteen women in the group, politely demanded. Silvia was a dark-skinned beauty in her forties who seemed outgoing and friendly.

"Through the following year, you will all embark on spiritual journeys that will expose all your shadows for healing to occur. You and your life as you know it now will be transformed. You will be reborn into a whole new being—one closer to the will of the universe and of God. You will be tested. You will be pushed beyond all your known limits. You will earn the right to develop great power and use it to fulfill your life mission consciously. You will be an instrument for the healing of all living beings. Throughout the year, you will receive tools; you will tap into a source of unlimited power. You will become a shaman," Simone said with a crooked smile.

"How can we know if this path is the right one for us? What if we're not ready? What if we don't like it?" Amber asked.

"You are here, aren't you? You are the youngest of the group, Amber. Don't you think that means something? At this point in your life, you are ready to receive this wisdom. Otherwise, the universe wouldn't have conspired to bring you here in the first place." Simone smiled gently with a loving look in her eyes.

"Many are called to this path; few will be chosen." Simone spoke mysteriously again after a few seconds.

"Chosen for what?" asked Victoria suspiciously as she accommodated her pixie-like black hair and turned her face to the side, looking doubtful.

"You won't understand until you are indeed chosen," answered Simone, standing up and abandoning the conversation respectfully. She didn't seem interested in providing the group with more information. "Let's take a break, shall we?"

Confused gazes were shared among all the students as they realized none of them knew entirely what they were signing up for. They did know it was a yearlong course in which the group would get together at retreats every three months. They would be taught how to perform healing therapies, but they would apparently go through a whole lot more.

The group dissolved, but Amber and Victoria remained seated in their spots.

"What do you think about this?" Victoria whispered to Amber, seeking comfort in her answer. Victoria felt a little embarrassed to have dragged Amber into something she wasn't well informed about and that they could regret.

Victoria was very thin. She had pale skin and colorful spiritual symbols tattooed all over her arms. Amber seemed way more delicate and feminine. They had met years earlier at a coffee shop where Amber used to write her novels, and they instantly became close friends.

"I mean, I don't know. We are already here. The teacher, Simone, seems nice and sweet. I don't think we would fall into something sketchy or anything. What do you think?" Amber gazed into the sun fading under the mountains.

They were all staying at an old house a few hours from the city. The house was large, and it looked like it had been beautiful a few years back. The walls were painted white, and every exterior corner was adorned with different plants, flowers, hanging trees, and shrubs.

It was in a beautiful mountainous area far enough to feel completely secluded.

"I mean, you know I would be interested in any kind of spiritual course that comes my way. You, on the other hand...Let's just say I know how out there this seems for you, and I would totally understand if you wished to leave," Victoria said in a loving and protecting voice, characteristic of an older sister even though they were just friends.

"Just because I haven't found my thing doesn't mean I'm not looking." Amber laughed, but her big green eyes glared at Victoria. "I've always been intrigued by spirituality; you know that. I just feel a little bit intimidated by shamanism. I feel like once I remember whatever it is I feel I forgot, nothing will ever be the same, you know?"

"No, I don't." Victoria laughed. "Does it matter? Let's just stay, and if it gets too weird, we can just drop out and never come back."

"Fine." Amber laughed, in awe of how Victoria always seemed to drag her into the most ridiculous scenarios.

They spent some moments in silence, enjoying the fresh weather. The night crept in, and it started getting a bit colder. The stars began to appear above the women, who were forming a circle again on the grass. All the women seemed refreshed and relaxed. The moment of tension had passed.

"We only have three more days to go, people. We need to continue covering the material. If anyone feels uncomfortable, please feel free to go," Simone said, inviting them all to reconsider the seriousness of the path they were choosing. "If you choose to leave, please do so before tomorrow's initiation ritual."

CHAPTER 2

"I'm so exhausted, I can't even see straight," complained Victoria as she unfolded clean blankets over the mattress. "I smell like barbecue."

"I know. Today was a crazy day. I can't believe how late it is and how early we need to wake up tomorrow." Amber allowed her fatigue to be sensed on every word. "I kind of enjoyed today, though. Loved the sacred fire—minus the barbecue smell. Learning about chakras was interesting, and starting to perceive energy was cool too. I guess I still find it interesting that everyone can develop these intuitive abilities. For some reason, I always thought you needed to be born with these gifts. I was relieved to know it's just a matter of developing the intuitive gifts we're all born with," Amber rambled, speaking mostly to herself.

"So that ritual thing?" Victoria asked while removing the dark eyeliner she used during the day in front of the bathroom mirror.

"Yeah, what's up with that? I wonder what that's going to be like. Hope we don't wind up in a crazy animal sacrifice extravaganza. Can you imagine? We need an escape plan." Amber said, in between humor and honest worry. "Although Simone seems so sweet, I don't think she would be into that kind of crazy stuff. I admire how much she knows about spirituality. It's like she has an answer for everything, and everything she says makes sense to me. You know?" Amber smiled.

The house where the course took place had plenty of bedrooms. All the students were assigned different rooms, and luckily enough, Amber and Victoria had a room to themselves with an indoor bathroom. Something about the house felt dark, though. They couldn't yet understand why it felt that way.

The beds were old, and the white paint on the walls was falling off on every spot in sight. The white luminescent lamps made it feel constricting, but they were too exhausted to mind. They showered and got into bed as soon as possible. Victoria felt her body heavy as a log and fell asleep instantly. Amber spent about a half hour writing in her journal about the experiences she lived throughout the day.

> Today was awesome. I can't seem to grasp what is happening, but I feel like this will be the answer to questions I didn't even know I had. Simone will teach us how to heal others. How to help people with depression, anxiety, and all sorts of disorders. I felt such a profound joy in my heart. I'm sick

of living in pain and seeing those around me struggle. I'm tired of carrying around such a heavy heart. My heart feels so heavy with a sense of grief I can't understand. I have no idea how I wound up here, but it's beginning to look like the exact place I would want to be. Simone said today that we will be working with spirits. That word terrifies me. I'm not sure what she means. She mentioned animal spirits as well. That sounds all right, but I wonder if she means we will be working with ghosts and stuff like that at some point. Can you imagine?

Amber held that thought for a while, feeling creeped out by the possibility.

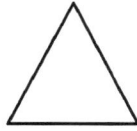

CHAPTER 3

Amber woke up abruptly as she heard the loud noise of the drums Simone was playing outside of their bedroom.

"Geez, what time is it?" Amber dragged her tired body out of bed and opened the door to find Simone with a wide smile and a lot of energy, beating a drum she held in her hand as she walked around the house waking all the others up. She was dressed in a long, colorful skirt and a spaghetti strap top.

"Time to wake up, Vic." Amber touched Victoria's feet gently.

Victoria dragged herself to a sitting position, her short dark hair was a mess, and she still had traces of the eyeliner from the day before.

Victoria was a bit of a rebel at heart. She was a skinny, tiny, twenty-eight-year-old astrologer who looked like a punk rock superstar. The tattoos on both of her muscular arms exposed how studied she was regarding spirituality. Symbols, sacred geometry images, and mandalas covered her arms like colorful sleeves. Her features were beautiful and her face delicate, yet the chin and eyebrow piercings she wore made her look like a badass. She was sweet and patient. Although whenever she got upset, you wouldn't want to be around.

Amber got into the shower quickly before she could think about how exhausted she still felt. Victoria started gathering her clothes over the bed; her body went through the motions, while her mind felt numb. When they were both ready, they rushed over to the study area outdoors. The group was already gathered, the eleven ladies sitting crossed-legged in a circle, awaiting just them. The group would gather over a spacious piece of land surrounded by beautiful ancient trees. All of them were ready with their notebooks and materials in hand, sitting over differently colored yoga mats and fabrics. They were all ready and excited to start the day, despite the dark bags under their eyes.

Amber and Victoria were just beginning to get to know the other ladies. They remembered Silvia from the previous day, the dark-skinned beauty with the warrior-like energy that helped them ask the right questions at the right time. The other names remained foggy in their minds.

Hours went by as they learned healing techniques, ancient wisdom, and sacred secrets from shamanic cultures from all over the world. Every minute that passed felt eye-opening and completely fulfilling to them. The magical lessons learned promised to change their lives dramatically. The way they all saw the world around them would be completely different now.

"Can you believe the things we're learning? Vic, this explains everything," Amber whispered in awe. "I felt it—the healing. I felt tons of negative energy pouring out of me, and I feel lighter than ever now."

"I know! I'm actually really impressed, I have to admit these concepts resonate with me so much deeper than many other spiritual paths I have explored. I felt different too, Amber. I really did. I had been holding on to so much pain I didn't even know." Victoria looked genuinely surprised as she faced Amber, whispering.

A sense of hope carried them through as they wondered how much they could possibly learn over a year if the second day felt this incredible.

"Thank you for bringing me here, Vic. I have to admit you did good on this one," Amber said wholeheartedly. "I'm pleasantly surprised." She looked impressed.

"I love you, little grasshopper." Victoria laughed.

They were both interrupted by Simone.

"Girls, you may want to pay attention to this," Simone said gently. "We are doing a lot of energy work. Every time we prepare the space for healing through the Sacred Space prayer, every time we encounter patients, and every time we explore our shadows we are using a lot of energy we are not used to using regularly. Every few hours, whenever you are feeling depleted and drained, have a spoonful of this mix."

"What is it?" Marie, another one of the ladies, widened her big blue eyes with a smile, showing how curious she felt as she leaned over to look. Marie was the oldest one from the bunch but looked young, inside a suntanned and healthy-looking body. She had long grey hair that went all the way down to her hips. She had freckles all over her face, and you could immediately tell, she was a very, very wise soul.

"Ginger and honey?" she asked with her mouth still full of the spicy mix. She moved her hands back and forth trying to ease the spice as she laughed, realizing she had way too much.

The group laughed and waited one by one for the mix to get to them.

"It is really important you guys drink a lot of water as well. The things we are doing here, your bodies are not used to. We are pushing the limits of our human experience, and if you don't take care of yourselves, you won't make it to the ritual tonight," Simone explained.

"Could you explain to us a little bit more about that?" Victoria grabbed her notebook in hand to take some notes.

"Absolutely." Simone smiled encouraging others to grab their notebooks as well. "You will all be receiving eight of the nine Munay-Ki rites available to humanity now. These are rites of passage that will individually contribute to your evolution into a Homo Luminous being, gently transforming you, one rite at a time, into becoming your most elevated self. These rites were initially shared by the Q'ero shamans from Peru. They are meant to be shared to allow humanity to evolve out of the troubled times the world is experiencing. They are all a gift from the heavens that encourage our evolution and ascension.

"Well, each of them will be transmitted energetically into your system, like seeds. It will be your responsibility to nurture those seeds in order for them to become all they can be. You will receive rites for protection, which will represent a sort of armor for you. You will also receive rites that will increase, awaken, and empower your psychic, clairvoyant, and mediumship abilities, allowing you to clearly perceive the world of spirit." Simone shared slowly, making sure no one felt lost in her explanations. After realizing everyone was following her, she continued.

"The first rite, which you will receive tonight, will be the Healer's Rite. It's also known as the Hampe Rite. This initiation will transform your body into a healer's body. After receiving this rite, your personal healing process will be accelerated, and you will enter a state of balance after getting rid of all limitations, fears, and emotional baggage you have been dragging around. Energy will be transmitted into your heart at the moment of the rite to facilitate a soulful connection with every single person who asks for your help, whether seeking advice or an actually healing therapy. This energy will allow you to connect easily to unconditional love. Energy will be transmitted into your third eye to awaken your spiritual vision and receive clarity. Energy will lastly also be transmitted into your Solar Plexus Chakra and onto your hands. You will become a channel for the healing energy of God to come through you and into your patients. Any questions?" asked Simone as she smiled, realizing her words got the whole group excited.

"Many!" laughed Marie as she got her long grey hair onto a high ponytail, getting ready to ask away.

"Where should we start?" Victoria said immediately. The energy of the group became lighter and nicer as they began to feel more comfortable with each other.

"Okay, I know! Will we feel different afterward?" Amber asked enthusiastically.

"You will probably feel like you were run over by a truck." Simone laughed, and everyone followed her in their joyous laughter. "Not necessarily because of the ritual, but because of the sum of everything we are doing. You guys are seriously doing so much energy work and clearing your souls from so much clutter, it is natural for you to feel a little out of it afterward. The ritual itself will bring upon you all sorts of sensations. It has been reported that often past life memories come in, leaving practitioners a little confused. You may have wild dreams, visions, and increased receptivity afterward. You will be able to observe how, in the following months after the ritual, people around you will feel very inclined to share with you their deepest secrets and issues."

"That happens to me already. Don't know if I like it that much." Victoria laughed sarcastically as she rolled her eyes.

"You may also experience a profound sense of coming back home. This is a sensation I can't explain to you, but you will know," Simone shared as she looked around all of the raised hands ready for more questions.

"Okay, so let me get this straight," said Silvia as she changed her sitting position. Her afro was stunning, and she looked so graceful while at the same time unstoppable. Her energy evoked a sense of powerful elegance that glowed out of her chocolaty smooth skin. "You are saying that by going through this ritual, we will be gifted with the power of healing others by hand imposition? Like Jesus?"

"All right. You will become a clear vessel and a powerful channel for the energy of ascended masters like Jesus, but not limited to him only, to come through you and heal others. It won't be that simple, though. You will learn the techniques required as well. You will receive guidance from Spirit Guides that will guide you into the facilitation of the ultimate healing for the patient," Simone explained carefully, attentively observing the students' reactions.

"Wait, wait, wait … Okay, let me get this straight," Silvia said, outraged.

The whole group burst into laughter at the way Silvia seemed to humorously use the same phrase again.

"I can't believe no one has asked this yet … Besides believing on the four directions, animal totems, spirit guides, and nature spirits, shamans believe in Jesus too?" Silvia asked, confused.

"Yes," Simone said, embodying the energy of a sweet motherly figure. "We believe that, God is one energy, manifested into different forms. Every god from the known religions not only exists but can peacefully interact with us. We believe there is no one way over the others. We believe there are ascended masters, ancestor spirits, archetypical energies, angels, archangels, extraterrestrial beings, fairies, elementals, dense entities, and earthbound spirits, among countless other beings, all coexisting with each other here on Earth, on different realms and dimensions. We believe in all gods, and we allow ourselves to work with the ones that resonate with us the most—the ones that feel right to us," Simone shared lovingly.

"Okay, I love that!" said Silvia enthusiastically.

"This is such a relief!" jumped Amber. "I have always believed in Jesus and Christian traditional beliefs. I genuinely believe in him, and I was wondering last night if this would somehow clash or intervene with my faith. I was actually terrified that I was, somehow … cheating on Jesus?" Amber laughed, embarrassed of her probably politically incorrect comment.

The whole group laughed, and before they knew it, they were all becoming friends. This was by far the most enjoyable part of the course so far. Everyone seemed comfortable, happy, and cheerful as they began to trust the shamanic path more and more. The unspoken tension was beginning to dissolve as they began to grasp the concepts.

"I swear I was just thinking the same thing yesterday!" Sonia jumped in. She was a beautiful Mexican woman in her fifties and seemed kind and polite as she continued. "I feel really comfortable with what you just shared, Simone. I have always believed God is one, manifested into different paths for everybody's preferences. I believe God is love that chooses to take different shapes and forms to satisfy us all."

"Yes, dear. We believe the same to be true." Simone gathered her thoughts, realizing they had fallen a bit off topic.

"This will be hard to explain to my family." Silvia laughed.

"You betcha!" said Victoria lightheartedly.

"You have a chance for one more question before we continue," said Simone, checking the time on her phone.

Marie jumped at the opportunity to asking a question and jumped up from a sitting position into a kneeling position as she raised her hand with a huge grin on her freckled face. Her messy ponytail began to fall apart, and she looked like such a stunning force of nature.

Amber gazed at her in admiration. *Damn, she is stunning*, she thought to herself as she admired lovingly how, even with her age, she seemed like a free spirit and wanderer soul princess. Her tanned skin was filled with freckles and barely noticeable scars. She looked like a surfer, traveler, and wanderlust who had probably searched the whole world for answers. Later, Amber discovered Marie had, indeed, traveled the world her entire life.

"How can you transmit this to us—the rites? What does that make you?" she asked, innocent and curious.

"Well, that's disrespectful." Greta said, jumping into the conversation. She was a chubby, short, and clearly short-tempered lady. "Do you know how much work Simone is putting into this? How dare you doubt her abilities to provide this rites on to us?" She answered, enraged.

"Wow. It was not my intention at all to disrespect you, Simone." Marie jumped back in surprise from this lady's intense reaction.

Everyone around the group became tense, and the vibe changed from fun to awkward.

"We are making tremendous efforts to put this together, and Simone is an impeccable channel for these transmissions. It offends me that you doubt her. She is a master in all she does, and we need to be respectful to her every wish. We need to honor her as our guru," Greta continued, making everyone even more uncomfortable.

"Geez, relax lady. I don't think Marie meant anything remotely similar to what you understood," Victoria said in a calm yet authoritative voice.

"What can you know? You are twenty-eight years old, aren't you, Victoria? You shouldn't even be speaking to your elders that way." Greta fired back, making everyone realize she had a lot of anger to heal.

"Okay," Victoria said sarcastically as she looked at everyone around with eyes wide opened, shocked at what just happened.

"Simone, I sincerely just wanted to know how it works," Marie whispered carefully, paying attention to Greta's reactions and trying not to make her explode again. "I don't know what Greta understood, but all I'm asking is how you got to the point of the process in which you are at."

"I know, Marie. Greta, we are here to learn. I appreciate all of the effort you are putting into helping me with everything, but I insist that it is not necessary for you to help me with much, let alone defend me from the assumptions you make. Marie was not intending anything other than receiving an answer for the question she asked," Simone said, starting at a high tone of voice and lowering it to make only Greta hear her words as they were sitting side by side.

Greta didn't say a word, and the whole vibe was just ruined. Everyone started feeling heavy and tired immediately. The vibrational frequency of the group was lowered radically, and they began to feel the weight of all the physical effort they had been exposed to.

Marie shared glances with Amber, Silvia, Victoria, and Sonia, trying to understand what had just happened. All of them looked back at her with compassion, feeling sorry for the uncomfortable situation she had just been exposed to. The group dispersed for a break, one that would be filled with confused opinions.

"So, Greta is awful," said Victoria in an annoyed tone of voice.

"Yeah, she's not the nicest, that's for sure. I'm sure she has been through a lot. It seems like she's really angry and looking for any comment to vent her anger," Amber whispered as she played with the blades of the grass they were sitting on.

"You will be great at that healing people thing," Victoria said, annoyed by Amber's compassionate answer. "Who does she think she is, saying she has some sort of higher rank than me because I'm twenty-eight years old? What about you? She must think you are the group's mascot at only twenty-two"

"Yeah, I know. It did make me feel uncomfortable when she said that," Amber admitted, looking down. "I have met so many older people whose lives are a complete mess and claim to be more put together because they are old. It seems to be the only thing they can hold on to sometimes."

"Yeah, totally. I know a few of those. Greta seems like the teacher's pet too. Didn't you notice? Simone went about her business, and Greta spent all day running after her, picking up stuff and helping her with things she needed no help with." Victoria stood up on the grass and stretched her arms toward the sky, trying to release the irritability.

"Yeah, I actually did notice that. I can't believe how awkward that was. Poor Marie." Amber laughed as she glanced to the sky, amazed. "I honestly don't care who I share this experience with. It is perfection as it is. I wonder how the ritual will be. It makes me kind of nervous."

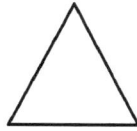

CHAPTER 4

"Are you ready? I'm hearing the drums already. Let's go." Amber grabbed her jacket from her bed and walked out the bedroom dressed in a long black dress and beautiful makeup on, which highlighted her green eyes and long eyelashes. Her brown hair fell carefully over her forehead, and her tanned skin glowed.

"Yeah! I'm ready. Wait for me!" Victoria closed the bedroom door behind her as she rushed to meet Amber.

Both walked rapidly from the bedroom to the patio, going through the kitchen where they'd all had a late dinner a few moments earlier. They were asked to dress beautifully and walk barefoot through the grass up to a hill behind the house. It was a mountain hill small enough to be reached in about ten minutes. The night sky was covered in what seemed like a million stars, and the coolness of the night had a sense of mystery to it. As they walked silently under the stars, Amber began to feel nervous about the ritual. Her hands were shaking and sweating. She felt a knot starting to form in her stomach, and she began having strong resistant thoughts telling her she still had time to leave if she wanted to.

"Vic, wait." Amber grabbed her arm, preventing her from walking any farther. "Are we sure we want to do this? What if our lives change too much? What if we begin seeing ghosts and it all gets complicated for us. What if we regret it?" she continued, feeling a sense of exasperation she hadn't felt in years. She felt panic rising within her.

Victoria listened to her attentively, looking at her with tender compassion like how Simone would address her.

"What if it becomes the best thing you've ever done?" Victoria whispered gently.

As they both stood facing each other for a few seconds, the sound of the drums became obvious again.

"They are waiting for us. Trust that you are being led here," Victoria said, putting her arm around Amber's shoulders and encouraging her to continue walking.

As they continued to walk, Victoria's arm remained around Amber's shoulders, giving her support. She realized Amber was shaking and seemed really affected by this.

"What is really happening to you? Is there something else behind this? You are shaking," Victoria asked, beginning to feel really concerned.

"I don't know what's happening to me," Amber cried. Tears began to flow down her cheeks. "I feel like something is trying to avoid this at all costs, Vic—something inside of me. I feel heavy energy around me, and I'm beginning to feel scared. This can't be good!" She stopped walking, released Victoria's embrace, and tried to clear her tears with her hands.

"What is your heart telling you?" Victoria asked, very concerned and seeing her strong friend completely broken in front of her for no apparent reason.

"My heart knows this is it. My heart knows that after this moment, I will begin to remember everything I feel I have forgotten but … I can't explain this fear," she said, confused, looking a little more put together.

The drums stopped. Complete silence covered the space for a few seconds, allowing the sound of crickets to become more noticeable. They glanced at each other again. The wind became stronger. It felt like the wind was encouraging them both to continue walking toward the circle.

"Let's go," Victoria said, leaving Amber with no choice but to follow her.

They walked into the space where the ritual would take place and were surprised to see the incredible scene. It was dark, only lit by big white candles—lots of them. Tons of white flowers adorned the whole space surrounding a big circle where all the ladies were sitting down respectfully and in absolute silence. The sky was clear above the space, and the stars seemed to shine brighter than before. They could feel a powerful magnetic energy in the space that immediately made them realize how intense this was going to be. A big altar filled with crystals, feathers, tons of incense, sacred items, pictures, and symbols of all sorts, laid majestically, decorating the area where Simone was sitting down, looking like a goddess.

Simone was quiet, her eyes were closed, and she was looking down with her hands held in prayer position. She wore a dark native shawl over her shoulders, which made her look like an ancient sage. Her body was completely covered by layers of fabric, amulets, and charm necklaces. Her blonde hair was adorned with feathers, which fell a bit over her serious face while she faced her hands.

The silence made the girls uncomfortable as they found their seats respectfully and realized everyone had their eyes closed. They sat there with their eyes closed for a while, wondering if they had missed something but realizing they were still on time according to the schedule.

The loud sound of a sizzling snake broke the silence, and they all open their eyes at once, shocked at the volume of the indescribable sound. Instinctively, some looked around to see if there was any snake around. A few seconds later, they all came to the realization that the sounds were coming from Simone, who remained seated calmly, exuding a fierce power and sacred presence.

Amber's skin got goose bumps from head to toe as she breathed deeply, trying to force herself to remain calm. Her breaths were shorter and shorter as a recording of shamanic drums started playing, although no one turned it on.

No words were spoken for the following twenty minutes. Simone performed slight gestures, indicating for them all to follow the beat of the drums with their rattles in hand. The magnetic energy increased with every minute, making them all enter a state of trance.

Amber opened her eyes and saw what seemed like a real, strong, physical wolf sitting next to Simone. She blinked in disbelief, and it was gone.

This is just too much, she thought to herself.

The smell of incense was carried all the way to her soul, and she felt lighter, sensitive, and completely alert. Her senses were heightened, and the sound of the snake's sizzling started again, sounding like it was coming from massive speakers, while it continued to come through Simone's barely opened mouth. Simone opened her eyes, and Amber's fear came back, rushing in and taking over her whole body.

That's not Simone, she thought. *Jesus, what the hell is happening? That is not Simone anymore. Who is in there?* Her mind panicked. Amber looked around to find all the other ladies with the same alarmed expression on their faces.

Simone looked physically the same, but her eyes looked different. The expression of her face and the energy in her eyes were not human.

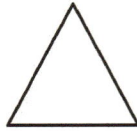

CHAPTER 5

Victoria grabbed Amber's hands, showing support as she could feel how Amber was completely freaking out. They interlocked fingers, and Victoria squeezed Amber's hand intensely, letting her know everything would be okay.

Simone's piercing stare looked directly at Greta, who was clearly scared for a bit but who seemed proud to be the first one to receive any attention from Simone. Simone's glare moved on, trying to choose who would go first and leaving Greta disappointed. Her eyes seemed to be sensing who was supposed to be the first to receive the rite. The look in her eyes was so piercing that it made everyone she looked at feel completely exposed and vulnerable.

Silvia was chosen to go first. She took a stance, proud and fierce, and walked to face Simone, sitting down right in front of her, like she knew exactly what she had to do.

How did she know she needed to sit down in front of her? Amber thought to herself.

"I think we are all being telepathic right now." Victoria looked at her with a mischievous smile.

Amber closed her eyes as she continued to breathe deeply. All the things she barely believed possible were happening right then and there. It was fascinating, and a part of Amber was enjoying it, but another part of her seemed to be trying to stand up and leave.

"Surrender." A deep voice said in Amber's mind. "Surrender, and you will find blessings greater than you'd ever dreamed of."

As Silvia was sitting, Simone would go through different movements and transmissions of energy on to her. Amber looked closely; some of the movements seemed familiar to her for some reason. She stared at a crystal Simone was using that looked like a donut. She later found out the proper name for it is a pi stone. Simone was holding, in her hands, her shamanic mesa, which consists of a blessed, folded piece of fabric holding several healing stones that had been infused with energy from all sorts of rites.

The mesa is the most sacred item a shaman from the Andean lineage can have. It is a physical representation of their spiritual path, and it's infused with the energy of their ancestors, their lineage, and all prior medicine men and women willing to assist them in their journey. Earlier that day, they were taught all about the mesa, and each had created their own. Amber's mesa was made from a thick Native American fabric filled with geometric patterns in yellow, pink, and orange colors.

27

Simone held her mesa on top of Silvia's head and flowed through several movements as she seemed to blow the energy through the pi stone and on to both mesas. By the end of it, Simone's hands were opened to receive Silvia's forehead, her third eye specifically. Silvia leaned over, and it seemed like Simone was giving her a blessing. Silvia seemed comfortable, but Amber couldn't believe she had to go and sit facing this being that seemed to be in possession of Simone's body.

That very thought made her hands begin to sweat again. The drums and the rattles continued carrying her deeper and deeper into an altered state of consciousness, and she began to feel dizzy. She felt angels placing their hands over her shoulders, letting her know it would be all right. She felt their loving energy cruising through her skin, relieving her from the worry. A few days prior she was in square one, and now, she could clearly distinguish angels by her side.

One by one, several of the ladies had their turns, and Amber continued to fade away into a profound trance. She felt like she could pass out at any moment. Then, suddenly, Simone's eyes looked directly into hers, making her jump in her seat. All her muscles tensed up, and her skin got goose bumps again.

"Your turn," she heard a masculine voice announce in her mind.

She stood up quickly and nervously sat in front of Simone, afraid to look into her eyes. When she did look, she found Simone's gentle stare meeting hers. She felt relieved, understanding that the teacher she loved and trusted was still in there. Simone's hand extended over her heart, and Amber's hand was placed on Simone's heart as well. She felt embarrassed of how her heart was pounding so intensely, and she heard Simone's compassionate voice in her mind, which said: "Darling, it's your time. It's okay."

Amber could feel drops of nervous sweat running down her forehead, as she continued to breathe deeply and tried to stop shaking.

"Do you remember this?" the masculine voice appeared in her mind again as Simone showed her the donut-shaped pi stone.

Amber shook her head shyly, letting her know she didn't know what he was talking about. Simone continued with all the transmissions, the same as she did with all the others. Every so often she would stop, show her a ritual tool, and the voice would ask her telepathically: "Do you remember?"

When it was time for the third eye blessing, Simone opened Amber's hands and place her forehead on Amber's hands instead, opposite of what had happened with the rest of the group. This surprised Amber, and she began to understand that perhaps that which she had forgotten was way more important that what she had realized before.

Simone came back up again and whispered into Amber's ear: "Goddess of the Water, Teacher of Teachers, I recognize you, and I honor your existence."

Amber placed her hands in prayer position instinctively and bowed back in gratitude to both Simone and the powerful being that was sharing with Simone her body at that time.

"Cuti Cuti Cuti, Nini Krini Nini Krini Ni Krini, Yoxi, Yoxi, Yoxi." Simone repeated these beautiful sounds out loud several times as she performed a protection ritual around Amber's body. These sounds resonated through Amber's soul. She could feel the sound of every letter bouncing back and forth in her interior so profoundly; it felt like it was protecting her past lifetimes and her future at the same time. She recognized these sounds so vividly.

Amber stood up, and when she glanced back toward Simone, she felt a profound sensation taking over her. It wasn't a nice one. She looked at Simone with pity, disgust, and a profound sense of disappointment. Quickly, Amber realized how awful that was and shifted her feelings and thoughts again into absolute gratitude for all the magic that had just happened. This all happened in a matter of seconds, and she never understood what it meant. It felt like a long time to her, though, as the barriers of time and space had completely dissolved in between the continuous beat of the drums.

Amber returned to her seat next to Victoria, who hadn't had a chance to go just yet.

Victoria stared at Amber carefully to see how she was doing. Amber's face was completely expressionless, which led Victoria to feel confused and worried about her. Victoria had no fear of going into the ritual herself. She had explored all sorts of spiritual paths, magic, crystal healing, and astrology. She trusted because she had lived a lot of beautiful initiations of her own, nothing this dramatic, though.

The ritual lasted four hours, in which they all felt so

high that their physical bodies felt a crash when coming out of it. An intense nausea crept into Amber's body as she dragged herself to bed. She smelled like incense, and her skin felt sticky as she began to feel the density of this physical world again. Both Amber and Victoria dragged themselves and fell into bed with the whole weight of their bodies, facing down on top of the mattress. Both of them fell asleep instantly while still wearing their beautiful dresses and without even moving the blankets on their beds. They fell flat and passed out.

At exactly 3:00 a.m., Amber tossed and turned in her bed. She felt like a dog was sniffing her face, so she moved her hands around, trying to push it away. She physically touched soft fur. Scared, she immediately opened her eyes and for a split second saw the beautiful grey wolf right there in front of her. His face was so close to hers; it was a wolf. His deep-blue eyes stared directly into hers in silence. Then, before she could admire him any further, he was gone; he disappeared, leaving behind the sound of drums in Amber's mind. She stared at her hand for about a half hour, in complete awe of how real she felt the soft touch of fur on her skin. She couldn't sleep after that. She felt like something was awakening within her, and it was the most beautiful feeling she had ever experienced.

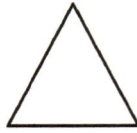

CHAPTER 6

A mber watched the sunrise over the mountains as she realized her tired physical body would never again hold her back from pursuing what her heart desired. She had gone far past her limit of exhaustion, and the human part of herself felt so small compared to the force of her "higher self" taking over—the part of her that is eternal: her soul. She wondered if the course was intended to be so intense that such things began to happen.

The sound of Simone's drums inside the house interrupted her thoughts, and she walked back inside.

"Oh, you're already up, darling?" Simone said kindheartedly, embracing her in a hug.

"Yeah, last night was so beautiful, Simone. I will never find a way to express how grateful I am to have had the opportunity to experience that." Amber looked into Simone's eyes with an honest intent.

"Isn't it unbelievable?" Simone continued to beat the drums and wake up the others.

"It certainly is. There are so many things that have happened that I want to ask you about. There's a lot I still don't understand." Amber followed Simone slowly into the rooms where the others were sleeping.

She found it funny how she and Victoria weren't the only ones who had passed out still wearing their dresses. She stepped outside of the room before Simone could answer. She wanted to give them all the privacy to wake up from their profound rest.

A few minutes later, Simone came close to her and whispered to her: "There's a lot you still don't remember, Amber, but it will all come back to you as we cover all of the material. I will guide you, and I will help you, because I can sense there's a purpose bigger than we know for the fact that you are in this group."

You would think Amber would feel special or more capable than the others, but in fact, she felt distant from those words. She felt like it rang true, but it didn't make her think anything about herself. She felt more confused and embarrassed than flattered.

"I really appreciate your support, Simone. I must say you are an excellent teacher. I find you really approachable and kind." Amber admitted as she leaned in to Simone's open arms for a hug. She felt safe with Simone. She felt like they had already known each other before, and for some reason, she looked up to Simone as some sort of mother figure.

They both smiled gently to each other, reassuring the connection that was forming naturally between them. They went their own ways as Simone needed to continue arranging her stuff. Amber walked to her room and noticed Greta was listening to their conversation the whole time and gave Amber a weird look as she passed by.

That lady is crazy, Amber thought to herself after feeling Greta's intense territorial vibe, like if she was jealous of Amber's conversation with Simone.

In the continuous parts of the course, they later learned, thoughts like that should be avoided, as all form of judgment contaminates our energy fields and lowers our energy vibrations. Plus, they are obviously unkind. They were taught to listen carefully to the words they used, the way they expressed themselves, and the perspectives they had allowed to enter their minds. Words, whether spoken out loud or used within our thought streams, are powerful tools for the creation of the world that surround us. Words can determine a big percentage of what shows up in our lives, whether it is positive or negative things.

After the lessons, many of them realized that day how they had been affecting their loved ones negatively through different unconscious behaviors—for example, by giving them advice they never asked for, by judging their actions, or by allowing themselves to fall into victimization. They all learned that manipulation can be an unconscious act and that they needed to enter a state of higher awareness and purification to continue learning these principles. They needed to develop self-mastery and a conscious method to protect their energy from slipping away through petty arguments, discussions, and negativity.

"Did you know about the Law of Attraction before this course? The one that says that if you are having negative thoughts, you attract more and more incidents to reinforce that negativity within you," Amber said as she grabbed her notebooks as the group dispersed for break time.

"Yeah, everything revolves around it. It is the building block of any form of success, happiness, or positive shift within you. Having that awareness is essential. Look it up; there's tons of material online about it," Victoria replied.

"Why didn't you tell me? I had no idea things worked that way, and I have been attracting all of those confusing relationships and boyfriends, issues with my family, accidents … everything!" Amber complained with a smile, in awe of how, now, everything made perfect sense to her. Victoria just laughed as she gathered her things as well.

"What else do you know that I should probably know?" Amber narrowed her eyes and looked at Victoria suspiciously.

"Well, let's see. Are you aware all physical illness stems out of untreated emotional wounds and blockages in your energy body, specifically your chakras?" Victoria said, closing the zipper on her washed-up old denim backpack.

"Yeah, Simone mentioned that yesterday." Amber stood waiting for Victoria.

"Are you aware that there are negative spirits that can crawl into your energy system and cause you anxiety, depression, and all sorts of crazy thoughts?" said Victoria, clearly trying to creep Amber out.

"I think I've seen that movie." Amber looked at Victoria sarcastically, hurrying her up so they could have a snack before the course continued.

"No, really. I'm not kidding," said Victoria, changing her expression from intentionally creepy to dead serious. "We will be covering that on the next retreat. They will even teach us how to extract those spirits from people."

"Wait!" Amber's green eyes popped in disappointment. "What?"

"Yeah, dude—serious." Victoria lifted both palms to face Amber, showing she was not kidding. They began walking toward the kitchen where everybody was having snacks and tea.

"Wait, what? So, you mean ghosts? Or spirits as in the movies where people are possessed, 'cause I can tell you right now I'm not extracting anything from anyone if that's the case," Amber said honestly.

"They will teach us everything we need to know. I'm sure it's not going to be like the movies. I understand it is a form of healing for people who suffer from these symptoms. I have heard we were made in God's image, so we are pure in thought and actions. I heard once that these, let's call them entities, are the cause of any form of addiction, depression, suicidal thought, murder case, rape, schizophrenia, etc. These beings are low-vibrating, dense energies that can come into you if you are not protected, and once inside, they will make you think it's you who is having these thoughts. It is subtle from what I understand. You don't realize they come in; you just feel like you have new tendencies for negative stuff in your life," Victoria explained, trying to make Amber feel more relaxed.

"Well, that actually makes a bit of sense. When I was dating Dylan, I knew he was bad for me in every possible way, but for some reason, I kept craving his attention, even if it was to argue. Looking back, I never understood how I could spend so much time beside him, knowing that it would never get any better. But there really was a small voice in me telling me to throw caution to the wind and continue with that relationship," Amber admitted as she glanced at the distance, contemplative of what Victoria had just shared with her. As she connected the dots, she realized there was an actual possibility this was real and would be included in the course.

They entered the kitchen, which was full of laughing ladies telling stories about their husbands and how they would need to take some serious time to explain how they were transforming into brand-new women based on the course teachings. Amber and Victoria served themselves some raspberry lemon tea, and they were all instructed to get back into the circle. They would be guided through a journey to meet their animal totem.

As Amber walked back following Victoria, she read the message on her tea bag string label, which read: "The path you would have never chosen is choosing you." She smiled, wondering if it was a sign and then suddenly realizing she wasn't paying attention to anything Victoria was saying.

They both sat down next to each other on the circle, ready to learn all about animal totems. While they waited for the lesson to start, Amber remembered her encounter with the spirit of a wolf the previous night. She couldn't wait to ask Simone about it.

"All ready to start, ladies? We need to go through this part, and then I will explain a lot about what we will be doing on the next retreat. It is essential that you guys continue with the course, even you feel resistance to come back. There's plenty of protection lessons you will need to know now that you're healing journeys are beginning to speed up. Even if what I tell you later sounds a bit scary, I need your word that you'll come back," Simone shared.

"Animal totems are also known as animal spirit guides. It is said that they choose you; you don't choose them. An animal totem is a helping spirit that has been with you since birth and will continue to be with you as your spiritual assistant, your friend and ally," Simone started as everyone opened their notebooks.

"You will be able to connect to them telepathically, in meditation, in dreams, and in physical form sometimes. They will always have your best interest at heart. They can protect you from all sorts of negative energies and spirits," Simone continued. "Each animal is a lot more than meets the eye. They all have a specific energy to them—an archetypical essence that can provide you with inspiration, understanding, and powerful abilities for you to overcome any obstacle you may be facing with your patients or with your own personal journey. Every animal has his own medicine. After the meditation that we will do shortly, you will not only discover which animal is your spirit animal, but you will create the connection and activate the relationship you will be sharing. It is also said by the ancient medicine men and women of this Earth that if you share with others which is your power animal continuously, the power in your relationship will be diminished. By sharing the sacred wisdom that comes from him to people who aren't ready to hear it, your animal begins to feel exposed and not honored properly. This will be a relationship you will need to take care of, enjoy, and cherish deeply," Simone explained joyously. "This is a very important moment for you all"

"I have a question, Simone. Last night I was visited by a wolf. Could that be my animal totem?" Amber looked at her with curiosity.

"Maybe," she answered. "Sometimes we can receive messages through all sorts of animals, but that doesn't necessarily mean that's your animal totem. They can be animal messengers. If you encounter an animal whose presence you find odd—for example, a frog found a way to get into your bedroom, then you receive an email from a place that has a logo that is the image of a frog, then you turn the television on to a show about frogs in Brazil—you can look up the meaning to see what is the Universe trying to tell you through the frog's appearance. The message you find online can be exactly what you need to hear at the moment, but that doesn't necessarily mean that the frog is your animal totem. You can just look it up like 'frog animal totem' or 'frog spirit guide.' Understood?"

"Yes, ma'am," Amber said as the group nodded cheerfully.

"Okay, perfect. Let's get started. Grab one of the mats and find a space on the floor to lie down. You will be all doing a shamanic journey to meet your animal totem. Simone stood up to help arrange the space.

Everyone found their space and lay down. Amber's body was sore, and the floor underneath her felt cold even with the mat underneath her. She closed her eyes, promising herself she wouldn't drift off on this meditation as she had done before on others.

Simone started drumming in a steady beat. She guided the group to visualize in their minds a deep jungle with a beautiful waterfall, characteristic of the country they were in—Panama. Amber enjoyed being guided through the lush vegetation in her mind, walking barefoot over a small trail and touching the ferns and bushes slightly with her fingertips as she walked by.

She began seeing the silhouette of what seemed like a black bird that appeared in between the trees, disappeared, and then appeared again closer to her like a hologram at fast speed. It would come and go so fast she could barely see what it was. She felt pressure on her head as she tried to focus her mind to see what the animal was. Then it clearly appeared right in front of her. It was a black crow. Amber's first reaction was to feel a bit disappointed, as she expected to reunite with the magnificent wolf she had met the night before. Then she observed the black crow with love, feeling like her heart began to expand and developing an instant, loving relationship with the mysterious-looking bird.

As he moved his head from one side to the other, trying to make eye contact with her, she felt like it was a long-lost friend she hadn't seen in a while. She physically smiled, and as she continued to lie relaxed on the floor, she felt a deep connection to this beautiful being, which morphed into a million colors and wrapped around her. It felt like the spirit was embracing her. She couldn't help giggling, and then she felt how all those colors, which were fluttering around her, entered her heart chakra. She felt ticklish and started laughing out loud, which made the rest of the group start giggling as well. Simone couldn't help giggling herself as she guided the group to come back from the meditation and to bring their animal spirits with them. Magical wouldn't begin to describe what this meant for Amber.

CHAPTER 7

At exactly 3:00 a.m., Amber started tossing and turning again. It was their last night in that room, which made her nervous every time she came in. They had left the white fluorescent light on because they both felt a little creeped out by the vibe of the house in general. As she tossed and turned, Amber began hearing the drum, as if it were time to wake up. She woke up and sat for a second as she yawned into her hands with her eyes still closed. She then stood up and walked to meet Simone, only to find out everything was dark and Simone wasn't anywhere to be found. Confused and still kind of out of it, she heard the drumbeat stop. The dead silence felt cold on her skin as she realized the lights inside the house were all out and it was still dark outside. There were no real drums being played.

"What the ..." Amber whispered, confused and a bit nervous.

I physically heard the drum, she thought to herself. *I wonder what time is it.*

She closed the door again and checked her phone to find out it was 3:03 a.m. She consciously tried to remain calm and not feel nervous at all. She tried to ignore the fact that every scary thing that happens in the movies for some reason happens at 3:00 a.m. She called upon her black crow for protection as she was taught earlier. She felt so nervous she called in the presence from all angels, archangels, and ascended masters she knew about.

Why am I so nervous? she thought to herself. *Why do I feel the need to call upon everybody like this?*

She lay back down again and felt like someone was watching her. She felt observed and alert. She closed her eyes again only to find the image of an old indigenous man in her mind with a mischievous smile that gave her no sense of comfort at all.

"Shit!" she cried as she turned to wake Victoria up, alarmed. "Vic! Vic! Wake up!" Amber shook Victoria until she woke up.

"What's wrong, Amber? What?" Victoria cried, alarmed by Amber's attitude.

"I don't know what's happening. There's someone here with us, in the room" Amber cried as Victoria gathered herself and sat down on the bed and looked around.

"How do you know? What have you seen?" Victoria stood up, beginning to sense the energy of the room as well.

"I see this old indigenous man in my mind every time I close my eyes. He seems evil and perverted—I swear that's the feeling I get. I don't feel safe, Vic. I feel like he's right here next to me," Amber cried, slowly feeling an even deeper sense of discomfort.

The fluorescent bulb began to flicker as if it would turn off completely.

"Vic! What the hell?!" Amber cried as she began to hear the drum in her mind again and the laughter of a masculine voice.

"Archangel Michael! Archangel Michael, remember? Simone said that when something like this happened, Michael is the one who can protect us," Victoria said, trying to remain calm and figure the situation out.

"Okay, what was it that we needed to do?" Amber breathed deeply, trying to follow Victoria's example.

"Give me your hands." Victoria grabbed both of Amber's hands and closed her eyes.

The fluorescent bulb was flickering so bad it felt like the glass would shatter any second. The tension in the room was so heavy and dense they felt like the air was too thick to breathe comfortably.

"Archangel Michael, we call upon you now. Archangel Michael, please protect our right side and our left side as well. Archangel Michael, protect the space in front of us and the space behind. Archangel Michael, protect the space on top of our heads and the space underneath our feet. Archangel Michael, we call upon you now to create a protective bubble around us and leave all harsh energies out," Victoria said out loud in a very authoritative voice.

The light bulb stopped flickering immediately, and they began to feel a bit more comfortable. They let go of each other's hands and started paying attention to how they felt. There was just silence.

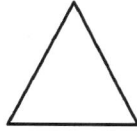

△

CHAPTER 8

"We have lived very intense days, haven't we, beautiful souls?" Simone said, drumming to wake them all up for the last time in at least three months.

They all found their way into the different bathrooms available at the old house, whose ceramic floor was beginning to feel dusty. The house had become home to so many stories, dreams, nightmares, and apparitions they had each experienced individually. Amber had memories she never wanted to forget, and the novelist she was, she knew that would never happen.

"There are a lot of activities planned for today. We need to make the most of it," Simone continued. "Let's have breakfast real quick, and I'll meet you in exactly one hour at the circle."

Everyone agreed in between yawns.

An hour later the circle was already shaping itself, as usual. They all had their notes with them, as well as their other tools and mesas. They had all bonded profoundly during the past days and experiences. They had worked in groups several times, and as they shifted partners, they all got a chance to create deeper connections with the rest of the participants. Naturally, little subgroups began to form, showing affinity between the members. Marie (the older, grey-haired gypsy), Victoria, and Amber had a clear resonance with each other, while the rest of the group subdivided in different ways.

"Today we are actually going to discuss a bit about the second retreat. You all had so much to share yesterday with the animal spirit guides that we didn't have time to cover it," Simone reminded them as a way to start the lesson.

"On this retreat, you guys learned how to keep your energy field clear by controlling your thoughts, words, behaviors, and relationships, allowing them to boost your intuitive abilities. You received the Healer's Rite, learned about shamanic illumination therapy, and explored your current and past life experiences in order to release all the baggage holding you back. You met your animal totem, and now you are about to understand your psychic abilities to a deeper extent. On the next retreat, we will be dedicating all our time to the understanding of dense energies, earthbound spirits, and entities of different kinds that can hold people back, sabotage their lives, and even create physical disease," Simone continued kindly.

Victoria and Amber looked at each other, sharing a memory of what had happened the night before in their bedroom. They felt disturbed by it; it was serious and intense. They both had nightmares in which the indigenous man appeared, and they had to continue to protect themselves in their dreams all night long. They were both exhausted and altered by the whole experience. Just as Amber was beginning to use the little energy she had left to worry, a beautiful black crow flew around the circle and stood right in front of her. Everyone in the circle welcomed the black crow with smiles, and Amber began to feel safe again.

"We will learn the second healing procedure, which revolves around extracting foreign energies, entities, and harsh spirits from yourselves and your patients. For this, we will have to face our fears. We will learn to protect ourselves and, most importantly, open our psychic channels to be able to clearly perceive these beings if they are around you," Simone continued carefully, trying to avoid ruffling any feathers, specifically on Amber who was clearly scared of the concept. Simone saw Amber's tired expression and just knew something had happened during the night.

"There's really nothing to fear. You will learn the principles well and will have those tools to protect yourselves and your loved ones." Simone then stood up and asked them to stand up as well.

"Gather up. You will be partnering with the person standing to your left. We will do a short exercise. It has nothing to do with dark energies—no need to worry," she continued.

Amber would be partnering up with Marie, who had her long grey hair in a high bun this time around, showing all the piercings she had on her ears. She was wearing dark sunglasses and a knitted top. Amber was thrilled; she loved Marie's laid-back energy. Even though Marie was in her sixties, she had the energy of a teenager surf babe. Her skin looked like leather from so many years of sun exposure. Her body was sculpted and muscular despite her age.

Marie smiled in a friendly way toward Amber, showing she was also excited to be working together for the first time. Everybody partnered up, and Simone shared the instructions:

"You will be sitting crossed-legged in from of each other, and your knees need to be touching. You will stare into each other's eyes for as long as you need to, and you will retrieve from your partner a tool for their development and a message for them. One of you must be the seeker and the other the receiver. When the first seeker has found what she was looking for, you'll exchange roles." Simone smiled and walked out of the circle quickly, avoiding all possible questions.

"What does that mean?" Victoria laughed, looking at both Marie and Amber.

"I have no idea," Marie said. "Let's see what happens."

Amber looked at Victoria with a sarcastic smile as she realized Victoria's partner was Greta. Victoria rolled her eyes and walked over to Greta, who had been waiting for her as she spoke to them.

Amber and Marie did as they were instructed. They sat down crossed-legged and made themselves comfortable enough. They both felt a little awkward spending so much time holding eye contact. Amber usually tried to avoid eye contact at all costs. She was very protective of herself in every possible way, and it was hard for her to trust others enough and open up that way. Later, she would discover that people with records of magic in past lives often report feeling ashamed or scared to look into other people's eyes due to their past life memories of persecution. They glanced at each other for a few seconds and giggled, finding it very uncomfortable. They tried again with no success until they both agreed to make an effort to overpass the feeling of vulnerability the exercise brought to them.

Amber stared into Marie's blue eyes and could see her reflection in them. She could see a mirror in which she was sitting crossed-legged, and there was a clear blue sky behind her. She could also see the green grass beneath her with some shadows and dark spots. For the first few minutes, she thought maybe the reflection in her eyes would start to morph and change, but what actually happened was that Marie's beautiful face started to morph into completely different human faces. Her focus was on her pupils, but the surrounding area was shifting; she could see it out of the corners of her eyes. She identified what seemed like Marie's past life personalities. She saw an old Asian man, and then it rapidly shifted into a black-haired old lady. It continued like that for the following minutes. It was very tempting for Amber to focus her glance on the new faces she was seeing, but she could tell they would disappear if she did. She focused on her eyes again and then saw in her mind a five-year-old girl dressed in a beautiful white party dress. She was blonde, and as she walked toward Amber, the girl gave her a little note. Amber opened it in her mind while physically continuing to stare into Marie's eyes.

The note said: "You need to slow down. You can't run away from what happened. You need to accept who I am, who I might have been, and how much it hurt you to lose me. It's okay. You are in the right space with the right people."

Amber tried to consciously remember what the message was as the little girl seemed to tell Amber to follow her. She sat down on a chair and said: "This is the tool she needs: a chair for thought. She needs to consciously stop and think before being impulsive about her life. She needs to sit down and feel the profound pain of not belonging anywhere. You see, Amber, Marie travels all the time because she feels lost. She always has, which is okay, but now that she has traveled the world, she still feels like she wants to check out of life. She wants to continue traveling, but this time, leaving her body behind. This time, she feels like she's ready to pass, yet she's not. There's something important still waiting for her here."

Amber's eyes watered, giving an immediate notice to Marie, who jumped with excitement as she realized something had indeed happened. Before leaving, the little girl gave Amber a small amethyst crystal. "This is the gift," she said.

Amber broke eye contact and brought her hands to clear the tears from her eyes. With a smile, she looked back at Marie in disbelief of all she had perceived.

"Wow! Well, that was something else," Amber said. "I have no idea if I imagined it all or if it's true, but I will let you know everything I perceived so you can tell me what you think."

"Okay." Marie jumped with excitement.

Amber told her everything she had seen, and while she was telling Marie, Simone approached them both and listened. Marie started crying intensely and covering her mouth, as Amber described the message and tool she had received. Simone comforted her. These where strong messages she had received—things no one could ever know. She had never expressed her feelings to anyone, and Amber had received the messages so clearly.

Later she explained that she'd had an accidental miscarriage when she was twenty-five. She lost her six-month-old baby girl—the only person she had ever loved. After that happened, something within Marie was irreparable, and she began her nomad lifestyle to bury the pain. She admitted all of it to be true.

Then Amber explained to her how the little girl gave her an amethyst crystal, and she broke down into tears again.

"Oh, my goodness. How can this be possible?" Marie cried, looking at the sky above her in disbelief. "My mother gave me an amethyst crystal on her deathbed. I need a moment. Can I?" Marie stood up abruptly, covering her mouth as she retreated into the house.

"Should I go look for her?" Amber asked Simone, feeling helpless and worried about Marie.

"No. Let her have her space. She needs it," Simone said.

"Hey, girls, I forgot to tell you that you also need to retrieve a gift for your partner," Simone said in a loud voice so every couple could hear her. She then whispered into Amber's ear. "Good job."

Amber exhaled deeply after the intense experience. She felt a little guilt for how affected Marie appeared to be.

What does this mean? she thought to herself. *Did I just communicate with the spirit of her lost child?*

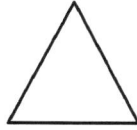

CHAPTER 9

"Sorry about that." Marie walked back from the house, looking a bit more refreshed. "It was just very intense. I wasn't expecting to hear anything even remotely like what you shared, Amber. That was spot-on. This exercise uncovered my darkest spots, and I guess I felt really vulnerable."

"Yeah, no...no worries. I totally understand. Take your time." Amber smiled and gestured for her to sit in front of her again. "Let me know whenever you feel ready to retrieve the messages for me this time."

"Yeah, I'm ready. Let's do it." Marie sat down and smiled at Simone, who was just approaching them again to check up on her.

"How are you feeling, Marie?" Simone hugged her from behind lovingly.

"Better. Thank you, Simone. It was just very intense." Marie laughed, still in disbelief but ready to move on.

"Okay, girls. Best of luck." Simone smiled kindly, showing a lot of support for them both.

Like little girls, they both felt nurtured by Simone's attentive care and started getting back into their positions to go at it again. They needed a few attempts again before they could get serious enough to make it work with the eye contact. Once they did, Marie experienced similar happenings. She saw Amber's face shift and change into one of an old Irish witch. Then, she saw her face full of scars and saggy skin, as if she had been a lady whose whole face had been burned in a fire. After that, she saw an old indigenous woman who seemed very wise and suddenly, behind her, appeared the blurry silhouette of the grey wolf again. In her eyes, she continued to perceive her own reflection and wondered, like Amber, if that was going to morph as well, revealing the messages. More time passed—about fifteen minutes—and Amber could tell Marie was becoming frustrated. They could hear how all the groups were finishing, and they were the only ones left.

Marie broke the eye contact and told her she needed to ask something of Simone. They both called upon her, and she approached them silently.

"Simone, I am not receiving any messages, but I started to feel a very intense pain in my heart. Like, bad. I'm not sure if I'm entirely okay after the first exercise," Marie admitted, looking worried and a bit embarrassed.

"Explain to me exactly how it feels," Simone asked curiously.

"I feel like my heart is made of lead—ridiculously heavy and profoundly broken. I feel a sense of desperation and intense longing for something. I feel like I suddenly can't handle any more heartbreak, ever. Like I just can't handle the pain in my heart anymore. I don't usually feel this way, and I'm worried what happened earlier might have opened up something." Marie looked up to Simone, who was kneeling beside them on the grass.

"I think what you are feeling is not yours, but Amber's." Simone looked at them kindly.

"It is embarrassing to admit, but I do feel like that on regular basis." Amber looked down as she played with a blade of grass between her fingers again. "Some things have happened to me. They have left me feeling so disappointed that I never really allowed myself to trust anyone anymore." Amber looking up at the two women.

"This seems like it's so much more than that, Amber," Marie said carefully. "It feels like lifetimes and lifetimes of sorrow and heartbreak. I'm afraid to say, what seems broken is not your heart but your soul. It seems like it's broken beyond repair," Marie continued, being very careful to not upset her too much.

"Nothing is ever broken beyond repair," said Simone as she hugged Amber for a long time.

After a few seconds, Amber began feeling the heaviness of her heart increasing and felt pressure coming up in the form of tears. Before she knew it, she was sobbing uncontrollably. Simone tried to comfort her with her embrace, and she started to feel Amber's pain. She was amazed how broken she really was. Marie couldn't understand how such a seemingly normal girl—kind, sweet, and productive—could have been living with such an intense wound within her for God knows how long.

Amber's crying didn't cease. It got worst. Simone waved her hand, motioning for the other ladies to come up to them and help. Simone continued to embrace her as the other ladies supported her by holding her hands and her feet. Victoria did Reiki on her heart as Amber began to have a full-on breakdown. It seemed like a faucet that had been closed for centuries, retaining all that pain, and now it had suddenly opened, letting all the pain she had ever felt flow out.

"Oh, my God," Amber cried in between gasps for air. "How can anything be so painful?"

She could barely breathe. She could barely speak. She could only cry uncontrollably. "Could anyone just take my heart out?" She laughed in between tears in disbelief of how horrible this felt.

Simone smiled gently and continued to hold her. "Just get it all out, darling. You can't continue this path if you are holding on to so much pain and carrying it around. You can't afford to do so anymore."

"But I had no idea," Amber said slowly, placing her hand on her chest, trying to ease the pain. She then began to breathe normally and started to look a bit better after a few minutes.

Amber began to recover slowly. She felt like a huge weight had been lifted from her, but she also felt the pain was still there. The feeling of being broken remained, and she wondered if it would ever get better.

As she sat down, Silvia brought her a bit of tea and some of the ginger mix for energy. Amber was covered in a blanket, and her beautiful young face portrayed the expression of what seemed like a tired eighty-year-old lady. Her green eyes were red from all the crying, she had bags under her eyes, and her smile was nowhere to be found as she contemplated the trees, feeling a million stories from the past rising within her. An air of deception in humanity surrounded her. It was too much of a cross for her to bare at this point.

Simone gave her some time and gathered the group again into a circle. After a few minutes, she called upon Amber to join. When she did, she sat in between Marie and Victoria again. They both held her hands and showed their support with a gentle smile.

"Sometimes, the older we are, the wiser we get. Sometimes we are also faced with the option of becoming very bitter. What just happened goes to show how Amber may be the youngest one here, but she may be one of the oldest ones of the group if we count in the past lifetimes and lessons her soul has been exposed to," Simone began. "You see, we have all had lifetimes of joy and sorrow. We have been both the killer and the victim in these past lives. We have been light workers, and we have been evil sorcerers. We have entertained so many roles, and we have created an imprint on ourselves—a karmic record and consequences with every single one of them. We have experienced duality and contrast through these roles. We don't need to judge ourselves harshly because of our pasts. This retreat is all about the "Sachamama" Archetype—the snake as a symbol of renewal. She sheds her old skin and allows her new skin to come forth, just like you saw Amber shed hers. Every death we have gone through in past lifetimes leaves an imprint. Every heartbreak clearly leaves an imprint as well," Simone said, looking at Amber with compassion.

"Marie, you did a good job on your reading. It wasn't as expected, but you opened the door for something important I had failed to mention. Every time we connect to someone with the intention to serve as a healing channel for them, anything can happen. Helping spirits, angels, archangels, and ascended masters can influence the outcome of everything for it to be as healing as it can be to that patient. We need to trust our intuition fully. We need to trust what we see, feel, and perceive.

"We all have so many layers. There is so much more within us than we realize, and this is just the beginning, girls. There's still so much to learn, discover, and unveil within ourselves. Amber's heart carries lifetimes of grief, loss, persecution, and betrayal. Her personality in this lifetime will be shaped by that pain if she doesn't release it. Just because it happened to her first, don't think for a second it won't happen to you." Simone looked around the circle as she spoke. "To love ourselves, we need to allow ourselves to heal, even if it's uncomfortable or difficult."

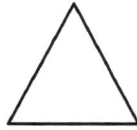

CHAPTER 10

"**A**re you sure you have everything?" Simone asked Greta who was holding her bags and walking toward the car to finish packing.

"Yeah, I think so," Greta replied as the placed the last bags in her car.

All the ladies had packed their cars and belongings, ready to leave and head back to the city, which was about two hours away. Some of them took the time to say good-bye to the beautiful patio where all the magical events had taken place during this first of four three-day retreats. One by one, they all started to leave, and Victoria, who was driving Amber, was still packing her bag.

Simone waved good-bye to everyone as they moved their cars out of the parking spaces. They knew they would be returning to a reality they no longer understood. It was bittersweet for all of them to leave. They would get back to the comfort of real life—their beds and their regular sleeping habits—but they knew that the most magical moments they had ever lived wouldn't be something they could share easily with others. Wasn't that ironic? Sometimes the parts of us that make us the happiest might intimidate or worry our loved ones.

As Victoria continued to fold her clothes, Simone went back to the garden with a cup of tea in her hands. Amber asked if she could join her, and Simone nodded tenderly. Amber fixed herself a cup of nourishing chai tea and walked toward the spot where Simone was sitting in silence, staring at the group altar. They sat beside each other comfortably without speaking a word for about ten minutes.

"I feel like I can trust you." Amber broke the silence, staring at Simone with curiosity.

Simone looked back tenderly and said, "It shouldn't be so hard for you to trust others, Amber. You have been through a lot of pain, but pain is optional now. You are ready to receive the lessons behind everything that happens, looking at it from a distance without engaging in the pain."

They remained silent again. It was a comfortable silence for both. They felt supported; they felt like friends. Despite the difference in their age, background, and personality, there was affinity within their souls. In a split second, Amber accepted Simone as her teacher. She opened her heart again for the first time and consciously decided to follow her lead, as she knew the wisdom she held. She saw integrity within Simone's soul, or so she thought.

Amber smiled gently and allowed herself to feel

TALES OF A SHAMAN IN THE MAKING

comfortable taking such a big step, maybe one she hadn't taken ever before at all in this lifetime. She had always put a thick brick wall around her heart to avoid anyone from getting too close. Amber stood up, placed her palms together in front of her heart in the prayer position, and bowed to Simone in honor. Simone did the same as they both smiled. Slowly, Amber walked back without saying a word.

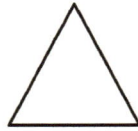

CHAPTER 11

Days went by, and Amber felt like something within her had awakened to such an extent that she didn't feel like anyone would ever understand her completely again. That ship had sailed. She observed people around her, and their lives suddenly began to look so simple. The depth she had been exposed to was unparalleled, and it was pointless to try to explain to others the impressive moments she had experienced. No one would understand. It made her feel distant from the reality that was so common for others around. She began to feel like a brand-new universe was revealing itself. She felt older, wiser, and more conscious than before. She could tell that huge things would begin to happen in her life—transcendental events.

Regardless of her initial opinion about the retreat, Amber had taken notes about absolutely every topic mentioned. She wrote incessantly, analyzing and describing in extreme detail what she had heard and experienced in her medium-sized red leather journal. The other ladies began to call her the scribe of the group, knowing that whatever was spoken would end up recorded in Amber's journals, for better or for worse.

Entering a path like this represented profound responsibility for every one of them. They were all given countless homework assignments they needed to fulfill before being eligible to go to the second retreat at all—to the second stage of the process. The homework included practicing the healing therapies on real patients, doing research, meditating every day, deepening their psychic abilities through exercises, and many other tasks.

It was weeks before Amber and the other ladies felt truly grounded and normal again. Their energies were shifting and changing dramatically, as were their psychic abilities. They all tried to balance their daily responsibilities with the huge amounts of work they needed to do for the Wheel of Medicine Course, which is the proper name for the yearlong process. Amber experienced incredible miracles during the test therapies, which were supposed to only serve as practice. The results she witnessed on patients brought to her constant reassurance of how powerful this all was.

A lot was expected from them. Becoming a shamanic practitioner wasn't something they would learn; it was something they all needed to earn.

CHAPTER 12

Amber threw some cold water over her tired face and then looked up to the bathroom mirror to see dark bags under her eyes that exuded frustration. She was exhausted, but she refused to sleep. A month and a half had gone by since the retreat, and she was pretty sure she wouldn't go to the next one. No amount of magic and wonder were worth this. Amber continued to hold eye contact with her tired self on the mirror when the sound of the coffee machine interrupted her. The black coffee was ready. It was two o'clock in the morning.

She sat by her bed with a rosary hanging from her neck, staring blankly at the floor as she held her mug in her hands. Her loyal cat, Paris, came close to her, showing his concern. He brushed against her legs and looked up to her with worried eyes.

"Oh, baby," she said as she picked him up and placed him over her lap. She petted him for a few minutes and accidentally fell back into an empty stare as she wondered how she was going to fix this. "It will get better, baby. It has to," she said.

Amber had spent the last two weeks having the most horrifying nightmares, apparitions, and paranormal visits from all sorts of disturbing spirits. She had performed every protection in the book, practiced things she found on the internet, and slept holding the Bible to her chest, but nothing seemed to work. The permanent feeling of fear was only overpowered by the feeling of helplessness she felt facing the whole situation. There seemed to be nothing she could do to make the nightmares stop. She surrendered.

"God, I can't do this. I'm sorry. This is just too much. I'm sorry for ever entering this path. I'm sorry for my complete ignorance. I honestly felt it was so beautiful, pure, and sacred. I never thought it could possibly hold anything this horrible. I was wrong. My path in shamanism ends here," Amber whispered, looking at the ceiling feeling completely hopeless.

The lights started flickering around her, and she stood up immediately, letting Paris come down her lap.

"Please, not again! I have no energy left to fight you! What do you want?" she cried, raising her voice. "What do you want?" she yelled.

The sound of drums began to play in her mind, and she held the cross from her rosary tightly between her nervous fingers. She stood in the middle of the room, completely hyperaware of her surroundings. Tears rolled down her cheeks, and her heart sank.

In front of her appeared the majestic grey wolf she hadn't seen since that night at the retreat. Her skin got goose bumps as she saw his tall, elegant, and fierce presence appear before her. His eyes were kind as he looked compassionately right into hers. She took a breath of relief and continued to observe him.

"They don't want you to continue your path, Amber. They know that if you do, it will be the end of them. You will eradicate great negativity from this world. You will balance the shadows of Earth. You will expose them." The wolf spoke telepathically into Amber's mind.

"You see, you are more powerful than you realize. You hold great wisdom within you from your countless past lives. You have lived centuries as a priest, a healer, a witch, a sage, a druid, and even an exorcist. Just because you don't remember any of that now doesn't mean you won't very soon." The wolf tilted his head, encouraging Amber to believe his words.

"These spirits you are afraid of will do anything in their power to keep you from continuing this path. They will try to scare you off, so you never reclaim your true power. Having you step into your power would represent a danger for them. These beings will try to keep this world in the dark energies of the ego. They are the shadows of humanity, earthbound spirits, entities, and demons that feed from the negativity existing on this earth. They know you could change things. They know your mere presence will bring light into all the hearts you encounter. They know, so they refuse to allow it," the wolf continued. "The path that you would have never chosen is choosing you."

He came closer to her, and she could feel his scentless breath over her as she remembered the same message she read on the tea string label a few weeks earlier during the retreat.

"The greater the mission, the stronger the resistance will be. You will face obstacles, Amber," he said with authority.

"I didn't sign up for any of this! I never said yes to any of this!" she cried.

"You did before coming here. Your past was only a preparation for this. This was the plan all along." The wolf lowered his head, looking at her kindly and silently encouraging her to smile.

"What if I had never gone to that initial course?" Amber complained.

"There was no possibility you didn't go. It was never your choice. It was in your divine plan, Amber," he answered back.

"Remember your power, project love, and darkness will disappear." The wolf then dissolved rapidly in front of her.

Paris, the cat, stood the whole time, staring at Amber and awaiting her next move. She was still holding the cross from her rosary in her sweaty hand. Amber sighed loudly as she sat down on the edge of her bed. Coffee was still warm, and the scent was strong. Her elbows rested over her knees as she dropped the cross and rested her face on her hands.

She thought to herself, *I'm officially going crazy.*

CHAPTER 13

The sunlight came through the white drapes, which were decorated with Christmas lights hanging over them. The rays of sunshine began waking Amber, who had passed out on her bed after her encounter with her spirit guide, the wolf. Her skin felt sticky, and she realized she had forgotten to turn the air conditioning on. Her bedroom was steamy, as the weather out was warm. She stood up to feed Paris, who had been meowing incessantly for the last half hour, trying to wake her up.

Before she stepped out of bed, she reached out for her journal. Her sleepy face and messy brown hair made her look like she had woken up after a long night of partying. Her white skin seemed paler, and the bags under her eyes were, at last, beginning to dissipate. She began to write in her journal:

It was the same nightmare, but some things were different this time. I found myself in the same space again, floating in the darkness. Evil spirits would surround me, push me, touch me, and laugh as I fought back. I could feel a scent of liquor, sweat, and sulfur coming from the ones I assumed where earthbound human spirits. These were all men—drunk men, at first. I remember how there was one who looked like a rotten corpse who floated right before me. He had no eyes, but somehow, he looked at me intensely. I was petrified and couldn't move at all. A force far greater than mine held every one of my muscles tightly in place so I couldn't even blink. I felt an intense pressure on my chest as I tried to grasp some air in panic. I tried to speak but couldn't.

That was all the same. This time, though, the nightmare had a different ending. This time I managed to say some words in a foreign language. It sounded kind of like Latin. The few first words I spoke were with a very low tone of voice. Then, as I got some air back in, I started speaking louder and louder, faster and faster. I can only remember the beginning of the words. *"Crux Sancti Patris Benedicti"* … or something like that. I began to yell authoritatively to this creature. Soon after, I managed to break free from the force holding my body immobile. I felt strong and powerful as I floated toward the creature who seemed to be moving away, still facing me. A force, bigger and stronger than anything I have ever felt, knocked me down and froze my body again. I remember consciously praying and thinking to myself: "Amber, wake up. Amber, please wake up. Please wake up!"

I could hear a laughter so macabre, I felt it was the end of me. I honestly thought I had already lost the fight. I began to pray as I felt this unprecedented force pull me deeper and deeper into the darkness. As he pulled me fast, I saw Simone, staring at the scene, motionless. I screamed at her to help me. I stretched my hand, but she didn't grab it as I passed by her. She smiled instead.

I began praying, I wasn't praying to wake up anymore. I was praying to God for my soul to be protected, because I knew where he was taking me. In a matter of seconds, I began hearing the cries of what seemed like a million broken spirits. They cried for help. They cried for forgiveness. They cried desperately for rest. The smell of sulfur became stronger, and I felt nauseous as he pulled me deeper and deeper into what seemed like the depths of hell itself.

"Enough!" I yelled so loudly that everything turned into absolute silence. We were both suspended in space.

"Do you think I don't know this place already? Do you think you scare me?" I transformed into some sort of wizard, and the darkness around me began to clear. "Do you know how many times I have come down here to rescue the damned souls you have manipulated into sin, into addiction, into murder? You know I have no problem reaching deep and far into your realm, bringing back what you have taken without permission."

She finished writing and closed her journal. She allowed the memories to sink in while her hands still rested over the closed journal. Her bedroom felt as heavy as her heart as she thought about it all. Her thoughts were filled with profound disappointment as she realized what she was facing. If it was indeed like her spirit guide the wolf had said, this was just the beginning.

Amber felt there were more questions rising within her than answers out there. She understood a bit of what was going on thanks to the guidance received by her spirit guide, but she couldn't possibly find the courage to face any of these beings in physical form in real life. It was intense enough in dreams. She couldn't imagine how something like that would feel in human form. She stood up, giving up the idea of making a decision about the second retreat. She didn't want to hear, dream, feel, or sense anything paranormal anymore. She had grown so sick of it, and no matter what her guides said, she was not going to that second part of the course. She was done.

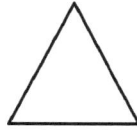

CHAPTER 14

"The payment deadline is tomorrow, you know." Victoria looked up to Amber as she rolled her yoga mat tightly over the wooden floor.

"Yeah, I know." Amber's facial expression changed immediately.

"Are you seriously going to let this opportunity pass?" Victoria looked at her in disbelief.

"It's not like I want to. I don't feel like I have a choice." Amber turned and headed for the reception desk at the studio.

"But you do have a choice. What about the wolf's apparition? Are you just going to ignore everything he told you?" Victoria followed her.

"For all I know, I might have imagined that. I was really exhausted when that happened." Amber lied to herself as she collected the payments for the other students.

Amber worked as the receptionist at a yoga studio in

Panama City and did her writing on the side. She had access to free yoga classes, and now that she was so tense about the retreat coming up, she had become a devoted student.

"Come on. You know that did happen, and you know he's right. You have to go!" Victoria insisted relentlessly.

"Vic, you don't understand. I can finally sleep. You have no idea how horrible those nightmares were. I didn't have just one bad nightmare. I had two weeks of nonstop nightmares. I would prepare coffee at two o'clock in the morning to avoid sleeping. I refused to try sleeping anymore. Have you ever been so afraid that you reached the point of thinking that never sleeping again was an actual option?" Amber explained, mocking herself. "I felt like I was seriously losing my sanity, and now I feel great. As soon as I decided I wouldn't go, everything got better. I have things to do in my life. I can't afford to go crazy, you know." She began to smile.

"Okay … I understand. I mean, I've never experienced anything like that, thank God, but what I'm saying is that even though you are dealing with very intense experiences, there's a possibility that was the worst part. What if the course is everything it promises to be?" Victoria whispered, widening her eyes with excitement after the last student walked out the door.

"Um, Vic. The course promises to be three days of lessons about dense energies and evil spirits and how to extract them from people. That doesn't promise anything good to me." Amber laughed.

"You have done all the homework. You know firsthand

how beautiful it is to help those you love and be a channel for healing. That is worth anything," Victoria continued.

"I don't know, Vic. What do you want me to say?" Amber looked up to her from the reception desk. "I know how beautiful it is to be able to heal your loved ones. Every single time I do a healing therapy, I feel like my life is finally worth something. I feel like I'm a messenger of God and the angels. I feel honored, grateful, and profoundly moved. There's nothing in the world I would love more than to feel comfortable and happy going to the second retreat. It makes my chest tighten to think I won't be able to join you and the rest of the group. It really hurts, seriously. It's just too terrifying, you know?"

"What if you get to the course and realize it's all easy? What if the nightmares were already the scariest part?" Victoria insisted.

"What if you are wrong?" Amber looked straight into her eyes for a few moments, which made Victoria uncomfortable.

"I know that if you are choosing not to go it's for a good reason. I admit I'm a little freaked out myself." Victoria finally gave up, allowing her posture to melt, which made her look weak.

As they walked out of the three-story building silently, Amber imagined the group going through the lessons without her there, and a knot began to form in her stomach. She missed the times when her life seemed so simple, when all she had to do was to cater the tasks at hand. Now, there was guidance coming her way, telling her the opposite of what she'd like to hear. Telling her she had to go all in, against her worst fears. Telling her she would encounter countless spirits trying to actively stop her, to scare her, and to push her away from that which she loved.

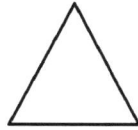

CHAPTER 15

The deadline for the last payment of the course had passed, and Amber had decided not to go. She couldn't get the course out of her mind—at all—for the following week. She wasn't experiencing any more nightmares, and the ones she had happened so far apart that she began to wonder if she should take a risk and just go. She called Simone incessantly for a full week, during which she got no answer from her. Her frustration increased as the final week before the retreat date was beginning to unfold quickly. Amber felt an intense urge to talk to Simone, just to be in her presence and ask her about the nightmares, the apparitions, and the messages she'd received.

Amber decided to call Simone one last time, and if she didn't answer, she would take it as a sign and confirmation she wasn't supposed to go. She sat on the edge of her bed and took a deep breath before dialing Simone's number again.

"Hello?" Simone answered kindly.

"Simone?" Amber jumped in her seat, realizing she was completely unprepared for the conversation. "Simone, this is Amber, from the shamanism course," Amber continued nervously.

"Hi, darling! How are you?" Simone seemed happy to hear from her.

"I have been meaning to contact you, because I have a lot of questions regarding some experiences I've had lately," she continued.

"Okay. Sure, darling. We can meet up today, if you'd like. I'm in the city right now," Simone answered.

"I'd love that." Amber smiled, feeling relieved.

"I'm free at three o'clock. Would you like to meet me at the old town for a snack?" Simone asked politely.

"That's perfect. Where should we meet?" Amber stood up and walked back and forth around her bedroom.

"Okay, meet me at the American Trade Hotel." Simone invited her kindly with a smile that could be heard through the phone.

"Perfect!" Amber answered with excitement.

Amber had so many questions in her mind. There was still a part of her that couldn't seem to shake off the words spoken by the wolf. She wondered if she was doing the right thing. She wondered if by avoiding her destiny, she would wind up in even more difficult circumstances. It was impossibly hard for her to consider going, but somehow it was harder for her to imagine life if she didn't go. No matter how much her anxious wondering took a toll on her, this had taken up all her mental space.

Regardless of how tired she felt about it all, she needed to find a way to feel at peace.

She had been diligent with the assignments and homework given for the course, even more so than some of the students who thought they would go to the second retreat all along. She woke up early every morning and did her meditations. She developed deep relationships with different helping spirits, including the wolf, which continued to guide her gently into continuing her path.

Part of the assignments were to perform healing therapies to those around her who would lend themselves and needed healing. She shared what she was doing shyly with her friends, the students at the studio, and her family. It wasn't difficult to get people to offer themselves for the healing therapies. It seemed like they could feel it was the right thing for them to do. Amber felt surprised as the months in between retreats went by, because even the people she thought would be judgmental towards her new beliefs would accept her help and admit their darkest secrets to her, in full confidentiality.

The healing therapies were beautiful. In each one of the following retreats they would learn a piece of the puzzle to ultimately become such a powerful channel that the healing light of the Universe, God, and helping spirits would flow through them effortlessly. It would flow in such a way that miracles could occur for the benefit of all patients.

At first, Amber felt resistant to perform this first procedure learned with her loved ones. She knew how she felt positively affected by the shamanic approaches, but she had no expectation for others to feel any different.

To her surprise, her patients explained to her how miraculous coincidences began occurring in their lives, pulling and pushing them from their original scenario into a much better one. New job opportunities, healed physical ailments, relationships getting better—these things were all beginning to prove to be common side effects of the therapies. Better circumstances seemed to begin appearing in patients' lives, guiding them into a sense of freedom they could feel at a spiritual level. It was a real healing experience.

Shamanic medicine believes that any physical ailment stems from an untreated emotional wound. It also teaches that we all have four different bodies all intertwined into what we know to be our human form. There's the physical body, which would be the one we know holding bones, organs, nerves, tissues, etc. Then there's the mental body, or container for our thoughts, thought processes, and patterns. The emotional body is the container that holds the emotions within our being. Finally, is the energy body. In the energy body, imprints accumulate over lifetimes—imprints of wounds, tragedies, hurt, ancestral karma, and any form of pain the person might have experienced. These imprints prevent the healthy flow of energy, which is supposed to occur in our bodies naturally for us to maintain a healthy disposition in all areas of life.

After we experience a wound—something very painful that happened at a given time—we will begin to digest it through the stages of grief. Then, time will pass, and we will feel healed at a mental level. After giving it some attention, we may begin to feel as if we have healed the emotional aspect of our memories about it as well. However, the energy body keeps that imprint unless it is cleared through energy healing or other methods aiming to achieve that release.

People will know if there's still negative energy regarding that particular wound inside of them if they find themselves being triggered by it. What happens to the body if a person thinks about the most painful memories regarding that wound for, let's say, two minutes? If the person still feels a heavy heart, knotted stomach, offended ego, or teary eyes after thinking about it, the person hasn't really healed. Maybe healing has taken place at a mental and emotional level, but that energy inside will continue to attract more of the same if it's not cleared. The more old baggage energy that's cleared from the energy system, the more a person is able to begin to step into his or her fullest potential and power. It is believed that the more these imprints are cleared, which can influence behavior in the form of triggers, the freer a person will feel to be who he or she really is.

Amber's patients began to feel this newfound freedom and couldn't help but tell her how incredible it felt for them. In their own way, they all explained how the session felt mystical and magical. Some of them shared how they'd had wild dreams in which they received closure for different situations they never received proper closure from before. Amber could see the difference in them clearly, especially in the patients who were the closest to her. She could also see her family members beginning to look more serene, cheerful, and balanced.

She knew this path offered an open door for miraculous and unlimited healing to unfold. This is what she was taught, but after experiencing it firsthand, she knew there was infinite power to the energies coming through because of these methods.

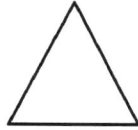

CHAPTER 16

"You are the only one who can answer that questions, Amber." Simone grabbed Amber's hand over the restaurant's table and stared at her lovingly. "You know what to do. Dig deep. Sometimes we fear our light way more than we fear any form of darkness. Maybe what you are afraid of is to realize that the wolf is right." Simone's blonde hair fell lightly around her aged face.

Amber stared deeply into the distance. Her brown bangs covered her forehead just above her thick brown eyebrows. Her green eyes looked intense and wise beyond her years. Her young face shifted sometimes, making her look way older than she was when she held important decisions in her mind. She looked tired, even though her skin was young and her face delicate.

"At what time are you guys leaving tomorrow?" Amber looked back at Simone who awaited her response for what seemed like ages.

"Nine o'clock in the morning. We should be there

around midday to start the lessons after lunch," Simone explained.

Amber's stomach dropped as she was suddenly reminded of the content they would be covering, but Simone couldn't tell, so she continued.

"Don't worry about the payment. If there's any part of you that holds the courage to follow your spirit guide's instructions, do not hesitate, Amber. Just call me, and we will find a way to figure that out." Simone invited her to reconsider her decision with a tender look in her eyes.

"If what the wolf said holds any truth to you, I will be supporting you through your path. I will hold your hand and guide you through everything you need to remember, learn, and discover about yourself. It would be my honor to assist you in your journey, Amber. I want you to understand that," Simone continued.

Amber smiled genuinely. She felt truth in Simone's words. She felt like she was finding a long-lost sister in Simone, someone who really had her best interest at heart at a deeper level than just human friendship. She could feel an ease to their interactions. Everything flowed between them, without the use of words, explanations, or physical behavior. They just knew they would be there for each other—always. They both knew it wasn't the first lifetime they'd shared by each other's side; they knew it wouldn't be the last either. They both felt an intense spiritual connection that transcended logic and allowed trust.

"Think about it, or better yet, stop thinking about it," said Simone as she stood up and grabbed her black leather purse embedded with turquoise stones. "Let your body decide. Our bodies are wise; sometimes our minds get in the way."

They shared a hug, and Simone walked out of the restaurant leaving behind a sense of frustration in Amber.

Why does this have to be so freaking hard? Amber thought to herself as she slammed shut her car door.

Amber had only hours to make a final decision—the most important one she had ever faced. It seemed obvious to her that she needed to go, but then she remembered the immeasurable strength of these beings within her nightmares. How could she possibly face them, see them, and remove them from patients' energy fields. Tears began to fill her eyes as she drove back home. Her stomach felt like a profound void, and her mind felt cluttered with sadness. She felt like she had finally found truth. She felt like she had finally felt God. She was exposed to miracles, magic, and possibility for the first time, and now, she felt it had all been ripped away. Immediately after she got home, she sat on the edge of her bed as she always did when she felt frustrated.

"Wolf spirit guide, I call upon you know ..." she whispered. "I need you. Could you please help me?"

There was no response, no drumming in her mind, and no apparitions.

"Please ..." she begged without an answer.

Tears began to flood her eyes again after a few minutes. She felt alone. She felt completely clueless in her search for answers, and she felt the profound sense of being broken again—the same exact feeling she thought she had released during the first retreat when an intense pain overpowered her heart. Her heart ached, and in a split second, she realized she had survived the disturbing hauntings, but she wouldn't be able to survive that feeling within her heart ever again. Now that she had experienced bliss, miracle, wonder, and connection, there was no room for that kind of pain within her anymore. Just like that, she knew. Just like that, she decided that she'd do anything to feel whole again.

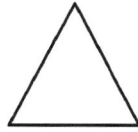

CHAPTER 17

The circle began to form after a half hour of cheers, hugs, and celebration. They were all happy to see each other again. They were brought back together to learn, share, explore, and continue to grow within their spiritual paths. They all seemed lighter, happier, and fulfilled. The bond that was forming between them felt like a safe space of harmony and love. Simone was delighted to have them back in her house for a new chapter to unfold. The grass on the patio was greener that time of the year, and flowers and butterflies adorned the space, making it a magical environment. They all sat down on their cushions and blankets, which were spread out over the grass on the patio space.

Once every one of them was sitting crossed-legged forming the circle, they realized they had to come a little closer to make up for the space that used to belong to Amber. Some had heard Amber wasn't joining them this time around, and some had no idea what had happened. Marie looked at Victoria, obviously concerned as she pointed to Amber's empty space, asking her only using her eyes what had happened. Victoria gestured back to let her know she'd explain all about it later. Simone witnessed the wordless interaction and sighed, disappointed to start the course without Amber in the group.

"Welcome back, beautiful ladies. I am honored to have you all back as guests in my humble home. I am most honored to be considered a capable channel to transmit these teachings on to you all. As you know, in this course we will cover a lot of material, so we will be very busy during the following three days. We will learn how to protect ourselves; we will learn how dense energies and entities operate; and we will learn how to eradicate these energies from our lives, from our patients, and from our surroundings, allowing our lives to become more peaceful and serene. We will cover four different techniques and procedures to help patients who are exposed to this. We will connect to the powerful archetypical spirit of the jaguar, and we will go deeper into our clairvoyant abilities as we prepare the ground for the third retreat when we will discover the magical process of soul retrieval. We will also be covering ..."

"Wait! Don't start yet!" Amber hurried across the patio holding two bags that bounced around her as she ran. She smiled, realizing how ridiculous she must have looked. When she finally arrived at the circle, she sighed in relief. "I want to join you guys," she finally said in between gasps for air.

They all cheered, welcoming her into the circle.

Simone held an unshaken sense of knowing and a smile. They all laughed at how dramatic her entrance was and how she hadn't even had a chance to leave her bags at the house. It was hilarious, but she made it. Amber left her stuff outside of the circle and sat down in her usual spot next to Victoria.

Victoria looked at her in disbelief with a huge smile on her face and hugged her.

"You came!" Victoria said as she hugged Amber tightly.

"I know!" Amber said smiling.

"You need to explain later," Victoria whispered as Simone seemed ready to start the lesson again.

"Sure," Amber whispered and looked for her notebook. During the break between retreats, many had even stayed in touch and asked her to lend them her notebook so they could copy her notes. She seemed eager and excited to start. Victoria was impressed and felt a deep curiosity as she wondered what had suddenly changed.

"We will start right away with the explanations about dense energy beings and their behavior," Simone continued.

Amber's moment of fun was quickly over. She swallowed loudly and began to feel her skin react to the memories from the hauntings she had experienced.

"As you know, here on Earth, there are nice people and ... let's call them unconscious people, right? By unconscious I mean rude, violent, discriminative, and overall imbalanced.

They all nodded.

"In the invisible realms, we have the same dilemma.

There are all sorts of beings, and you guys need to understand how to identify them, communicate to them, and protect yourselves from them, if necessary. Helping spirits can be your allies, guides, and friends. They can provide for you healing, teachings, and information about your patients.

"You will be going through several new rites, and they will prepare you to see the invisible world of energies. Spirits will know you can see them, and they will come to you for help, assistance, or sometimes selfish agendas. It is completely understandable if you feel afraid. It is not acceptable, however, to allow the fear to come in the way. Am I right, Amber?" Simone said, feeling proud of her for her decision to show up.

"The first chapter will be covering the healing aspect of extraction therapy, which is the first procedure we will learn on this retreat. Currently, it is common to experience anxiety, depression, and all forms of mental illnesses because of the disconnection to nature. Modern medicine as we know it is a recent subject. Back in the day, there were no pills. Instead, there was energy medicine from the indigenous communities of the world. If your soul is healthy, your body will mirror that. The healthier the state of your soul and spirit, the healthier your body and life. The shamanic path teaches that many ailments, addictions, and negative scenarios may be caused by low vibration beings entering our systems," Simone explained.

"Why would they want to enter our systems, Simone? That's the part I don't understand," Victoria asked.

"Because you guys have a human body. They don't.

Some of them are earthbound spirits who can't yet understand they have died. Some others are entities that feed from dense energies, and you guys serve as hosts, through whom they can experience life again and be fed and supported. Entities will feed from dense energies you feel, so once they enter your system, like a virus on a computer, they begin to mess with your head to make you produce negativity and, thereby, feed themselves through it. When that happens, suddenly, you are more anxious than ever. Suddenly, all the decisions you make lead you to disappointment, anger, frustration, or rage, which will ultimately feed these beings.

"They are capable of manipulating you by placing negative thoughts, perspectives, and images in your mind that will ultimately lead you to develop all sorts of fears, confusion, and assumptions."

"Years?" Amber asked, intrigued. "So, you can have them for years without knowing?"

"Yes, darling, they can come in at a certain point in your life and guide you into depleting the rest of it.

"Observe the world around you, guys. Observe it with an objective point of view, knowing that no matter how disturbing the things you discover may be, balance is always restorable. Observe the system in which we live in. As you progress on your spiritual path and focus on keeping your energy high, you will discover it seems like the whole world is designed to prevent that from happening. You will find out that everything seems to be contaminated. Television shows, news, popular song lyrics, GMO foods, politicians, wars, you name it. Even the drugs that are legal, which are way more harmful than some that are illegal, are a proof that we are living in a time of spiritual war. We should avoid focusing on the negative, but we must open our eyes to this reality as well, even just for a bit.

"Alcohol is one of the easiest ways for our energy to drop into lower vibrations and become vulnerable to entities coming in. Marijuana promotes connection to spiritual awareness, as well as some other drugs that are considered illegal. The drugs that could promote connection to higher awareness are frowned upon by society, while those that open the doors to these beings are promoted and encouraged. The physical repercussions of being drunk are way worse than the repercussions of being high. People die daily because of drunken accidents, but somehow, alcohol is a multimillion dollar industry," Simone explained.

"The system seems to be designed to break our souls apart, pulling us further into unsustainable materialism and destroying our only potential savior: nature. Are you are aware, the water we consume and almost every single brand of toothpaste includes fluoride in it. Fluoride is the chemical that affects overall health of the pineal gland in the brain, also known as our third eye."

"Wow, really?" Silvia's black eyes widened as she realized what Simone said resonated profoundly within her

"Who's controlling this?" Marie said. "There has to be someone behind these decisions. I can't agree with you more. As women, we are almost forced into hating our bodies, as well as our curves, our grey hair, and our wrinkles. As men, they are expected to expose such a deal of responsibility as the household leader, and the only way they can do it is by giving into ridiculous schedules and tons of stress. And they will ultimately release stress in the worst ways too—the ones that are socially accepted, like drinking, smoking, being violent, or just becoming depressed enough to turn to antidepressants."

"My point, exactly," Simone responded. "I can't know who is behind it, but I do know there are many people in high places who have entities within their systems and don't know it. Some others know it all too well. It's not their fault either. They are, to a certain extent, victims of this, and all of the socially acceptable behaviors feed them"

"This is crazy." Victoria looked at Simone, feeling overwhelmed and disappointed.

"I know, darling. This is not meant to discourage you, though. We have a lot of work to do if we plan to restore the balance on Earth. You will be trained to make a huge difference in this world. I just want you to understand that a person who acts in any harmful way is probably influenced by some kind of negative energy within his or her system. As humans, we are extensions of God. We were created in the likeness of God. As human beings, we are loving in nature, kind, and open.

"The thing is, we've all been hurt in different ways. Some of us have just been educated this way, misinformed, and overall asleep enough not to notice. Some of us are strong enough to hold these foreign energies within our systems yet live happy and healthy lives. Others are so hurt to begin with that those energies take over and take advantage of their vulnerability. After you begin to see the clear symptoms in the people around you, you will allow yourself to become more compassionate toward others. We are all a sum of many of our imprints, but entities have a profound effect on a person's personality, as you will come to understand after feeling how they will be extracted from your energy systems."

"Wait ... You mean we have entities too?" Amber asked.

"Of course. You all do," Simone assured as they exchanged confused looks.

"Don't you think we would know?" Amber insisted.

"Oh, darling, they can be so sneaky." Simone looked at her compassionately. "Their voices are completely intertwined with the ones from your thoughts. When they speak, you will hear your own voice in your mind. You will be led to believe these are your thoughts."

"So, any form of negative thought can be blamed on entities?" Silvia asked as she covered her arms with a natural insect repellent.

"No. As you begin to monitor your thoughts, you will become more familiarized with positive and negative thoughts. You will also learn how sometimes we fall into a victim mentality. Astrology has a strong influence on the way we think and feel at any given day as well. So, it's not just this, it could be many things. You will learn how gratitude can shift that train of thought immediately. This takes some time to master, but everybody can learn how to master their thoughts. If you feel, however, that something within you is actively trying to keep you swimming in negative thoughts against your conscious efforts, for prolonged periods of time, that could probably be blamed on some form of dense energy within your system. The way they operate within your system is very subtle. They don't want to be noticed. They want to make you think it's you who is feeling that way. They will, over the years, make you believe it is you who is flawed, guiding you away from your highest truth, which is your infinite power and love," Simone explained carefully, trying to keep them all clear.

"Oh," Amber sighed. "Now I understand."

"Have you experienced anything like it?" Simone asked.

"Yes, many times. I remember right before walking toward the Healer's Rite, I had a bit of a panic attack, and that was exactly what I felt—like something inside of me needed me to walk the other way. All of my fears intensified, and if it wasn't for Vic, I would have never received the blessings to become a healer."

"I actually think I know what you mean." Silvia spoke again. "Sometimes I know what I need to do but feel an intense resistance to it—like there was something within me wishing to see me fail or make the wrong decision. I feel like I'm constantly fighting something within me to be a functional human being."

"Exactly. It could be due to a foreign energy in your system or, it could also be due to your own subconscious programming. But today we will be focusing on how these entities can intensify our already existing fears. Those are the ways in which they try to manipulate us. This is something that will be covered in depth here in the Wheel of Medicine Course later. If I want you to take anything from this explanation, it's that just because a person is acting out, suffering from mental illnesses, or exhibiting crazy behavioral patterns, that doesn't mean they are unlovable, mean, or condemned to continue being this way. Everything is reversible, and absolutely everything can be healed through shamanic medicine. We all deserve to be happy, complete, and inspired in our lives. Some people may be incapable of feeling that way right now, but that doesn't mean they can't enter a state of complete happiness down the road. You will need to look at everyone differently now, as sacred beautiful beings who simply may be dealing with difficult realities at this point."

"So, are shamans the only ones who know about this?" Silvia asked

"No, not at all. In almost all forms of energy healing therapies, negative influences are acknowledged with different names and addressed through different procedures. You will treat patients who will be suffering from all sorts of imbalances like suicidal thoughts, extreme compulsion, anxiety, depression, sabotage, and mental disorders. These symptoms can all be healed within one or two sessions through extraction therapy. Further ahead after graduating, you will discover that helping spirits can extract these beings from you, directly, without the use of an intermediary or practitioner," Simone said.

"Wow, really?" Amber's eyes lit up with curiosity.

"Yeah, I receive energy clearings from archangels directly all the time. They can do for you all the techniques you will be learning here and anything else they consider appropriate for your healing process. They are capable of doing things you couldn't even imagine." Simone began to smile. "In the meantime, you will receive an extraction therapy from your fellow students.

"This is just the start of the journey for you. Your mind will continue to expand further and further to accommodate all of the incredible things you will experience. You will begin doing things you didn't think humans could do." Simone placed both of her hands, one on top of the other, over her heart as she smiled in excitement.

"This is just the beginning, ladies. You will continue to get closer and closer to a state of Ayni—of bliss and complete balance. You will continue to remove all of the baggage and begin to turn into your most beautiful, happy, and authentic self."

"If we make it through this part," whispered Victoria, trying to be funny but making it apparent to the rest of the group how intimidated she was.

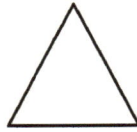

CHAPTER 18

Amber was paired up with Greta for the first extraction therapy. They had a few hours to prepare. Simone taught them how to protect themselves from absorbing any harsh energies from their patients. After all the preparations, they were ready to begin. It was nighttime already, and the stars adorned the sky. The scent of white rose incense provided an air of familiarity and serenity.

Greta decided she could do it first. That way Amber could see how she did it and learn from it, according to her. Greta dispelled this air of superiority in a very subtle way. It seemed to get on everyone's nerves, but not Amber's—not yet at least. Greta had never done an extraction therapy before, so they were both at ground zero; however, Greta was convinced that because she was older, she knew better. Amber didn't mind at all. She began to see her with more compassion and began to go along with her comfortably to make sure Greta was at peace.

The therapy was supposed to take about fifteen minutes. It would start with a physical muscle test to verify if the patient was indeed hosting some shape or form of foreign energy within her system. The muscle test was foolproof and really easy to perform, and both of them had their notes nearby to remind them the order of the steps. If the muscle test was positive, then they would go through a process in which they aimed to transfer that energy toward a special crystal that was held between both of their hands, thereby allowing the patient to be freed from it.

Greta began confidently, and the muscle test proved Amber was indeed hosting some kind of entity within her system. Greta continued quickly and wasn't paying attention to her notes. She moved past every movement, and Amber began to realize she wasn't doing it in the proper order they had been taught.

"Greta, I think you skipped a step," Amber whispered politely, afraid of Greta's reaction but even more afraid of suffering the consequences of her mistakes during such a procedure.

"No, I'm good," she insisted.

Amber began becoming irritated with her. *This lady is something else,* she thought to herself as a bit of anger began to rise within her. She was already scared going through it, and Greta's attitude didn't make her feel any better.

Amber breathed deeply and surrendered to the experience.

"All done!" Greta said enthusiastically.

"Already? That's great!" Amber said, surprised she didn't feel a thing.

"Let's do the muscle test, and we are done." Greta began to pick up her stuff confidently.

They repeated the muscle test, and it still showed the foreign energy remained inside Amber's system.

"Oh. Hmm … Wait, Amber. I think we aren't done yet," Greta whispered, surprised at the result of the test. "Let's do it again."

"Greta, there's a step you are mixing up. I have it here in my notes," Amber whispered politely again.

Greta looked at Amber's papers and without saying a word continued to go through the therapy. All Amber could think about is how she felt sorry for any of Greta's future patients, as she seemed like the most cold and stubborn practitioner in the world.

They repeated the whole procedure only to find out it was unsuccessful. They called on Simone to come help, and she guided Greta silently step by step up to the point when Amber was completely entity free. Amber's fear was defeated by the impatience that had built up after several failed attempts. She had grown tired of the process and had memorized every step at that point.

When it was her turn to extract Greta's entities, her nerves began to kick in again. She felt a little weak in the knees, and her hands were sweaty. She went through the steps carefully and placed all her attention on the procedure, to such a point that she almost forgot what she was trying to do. She gave no importance to the entity and just went through the motions. To her surprise, she got the energy out in her first attempt. After the muscle test confirmed it at the end, Amber celebrated and looked at Simone who seemed pleasantly surprised as well. Amber couldn't believe it. It was so easy. It was so much easier than any of the nightmares she experienced. It was seriously not a big deal. Amber's relief was huge, as she had been fearing this moment ever since the first time she heard about these beings.

"Great! That was perfect!" Simone said. "See, it wasn't that scary, right? I will discuss a bit about what happened here with the group if that's okay." Simone patted them each on the back and headed back to her spot on the circle.

Amber and Greta were uncomfortable around each other. They could both feel tension and a sense of rejection against the other. Both tried to be polite, but they both knew that they were pretending. They separated and each went to her seat as they waited for all the groups to finish and come back to the circle.

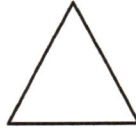

CHAPTER 19

The group gathered slowly, showing how tired they were already. A lot of them reported feeling like a huge weight was lifted off their shoulders. They all felt scared before the extraction therapy procedure, whether they would admit it or not, and having that part of the process covered gave them a big relief.

"Welcome back, powerful light workers!" Simone said joyously as she looked at their relieved faces. "We have gone through one of the biggest bumps of these whole course right now. You have faced your fears and interacted, communicated, and extracted harsh entities tonight. You should all feel very proud of yourselves." She lit a bundle of six incense sticks and allowed the smoke to clear the space.

"I know there are a lot of questions coming up about all of your experiences, and I want to take some time to answer them all to make sure we are all on the same page. Before we do that, I wanted to share with you something that was experienced by many of the practitioners." Simone stared directly at Greta.

"Many of us were trying to overpower the entities in order to obligate them to come out. As I mentioned earlier, we need to be strong and authoritative; however, our true strength will come if we emanate the energy of love, not of fear. No matter how perfectly you do each step, if you do it feeling fear, you become weaker and more vulnerable. If, instead, you look at this creature with compassion, love, and a calm sense of authority, not only will it listen to you, but it will fear you and your powerful capacity of feeling love even when it might be trying to scare you of. Love is strength," Simone explained.

"As we explained before, you need to communicate with them and convince them to leave the patient's system. When you do this, you will know more about the nature of that being. Having that said, I want to know a bit about your experiences."

Simone handed her talking stick, which was decorated with colorful feathers, beads, and crystals, to Silvia for her to have the space for sharing her experience.

"To my surprise, the being actually seemed sweet and confused. I could sense it was a feminine energy, maybe of a human woman who had died. She would insist she had no idea what was going on. I explained to her politely, to the best of my abilities, until she voluntarily guided herself to the crystal. I was ready for a war to go down, and she was so sweet. It was really confusing." Silvia laughed and looked at the others, who began to laugh as well.

"That probably means it was an earthbound spirit who accidentally wound up in your patient's system. Remember, ladies, that the story behind it is not important. What is important is to get whatever is in there out effectively," Simone answered.

Silvia passed the talking stick to Victoria, who seemed very energetic and cheerful.

"Okay, so what happened to me was kind of similar to what happened to Silvia. The dialogue was not scary at all. It was easy. What shocked me was the feeling I got when the entities was pulled out of me when it was my turn to be the patient. I felt the strangest sensation. I felt like a thick liquid was coming out of me. It was so bizarre! It was awesome!" Victoria grabbed her notebooks tightly to her chest, looking at the sky and appearing to be as excited as her body would allow her.

They all laughed at her hilarious form of expression. Next, Victoria handed the talking stick to Amber.

"Well, there was no internal dialogue with mine. Mine was not polite at all, though. It was one of those evil beings I had seen in the nightmares. He looked like a weird ghost, and I could sense how he was trying to scare me. I never engaged in conversation with him. I just expanded my heart center, projecting love outward, and he had no choice. He had no way of avoiding it. He was scared as he was pulled into the crystal." Amber shared with the group. "I can't say I enjoyed it, but it was way easier than what I had imagined it to be."

"Amber, that is amazing," Simone said, surprised by her story. "You had one of the tough ones. In that case, ladies, that was not an earthbound spirit. That was a harsh entity. I think those nightmares were preparing you. Entities can shift forms to find what would scare the practitioner the most. What she did with her heart and love energy is exactly what I meant. They don't stand a chance against you if you do that. You take all of their power away without the need to be rude to them. Good for you, Amber," Simone continued, looking surprised.

Greta's energy grew darker, and Amber could feel her density starting to spread over the circle like a cloud. Amber had no idea how Greta wound up being so bitter. She continuously wondered if she had gone through some kind of tragedy that made her create a thick, defensive barrier, leaving everyone else out for protection.

Amber was so excited and happy to have overcome her fears that she didn't give Greta any further attention. She had made it, and that was all that mattered to her. The relief she felt increased by the minute as she realized she would be able to go through all the beautiful parts of the course that would follow this challenge. She felt grateful, expansive, and inspired. She couldn't wait to see her spirit guide again, the wolf, and share with him that she had not only gone to the retreat, but she did the extraction.

Nobody enjoyed this part, but what was coming afterward would give peace to their spirits in ways they had never experienced before. Amber had found peace already by knowing that what she feared most didn't stand a chance against her. It was a good day. It was the best day.

The women loved each other's company at this point. They had all finally found a space in which they could be completely authentic. It was a night of celebration for all of them as they realized they had been freed from their own issues and helped one of their friends in the process as well. They gathered for hours around the sacred fire, listening to the night sounds of crickets, crackling wood, and flames. The stars delighted their view of the heavens, and the forest enjoyed the sound of their laughter.

They felt accompanied by the spirits of nature, peacefully sharing the space with them. They could feel the presence of magic, of fairies, and of elemental spirits. Their hearts felt expansive as they held colorful dreams and gratitude for the way they had all been guided to walk this path together.

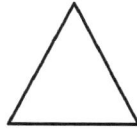

CHAPTER 20

"**I** have never been so happy in my life, Vic." Amber's smile was huge and her expression hilarious.

Victoria smiled gently and wrapped her arms around her, laughing at her ridiculous expression.

"I'm so happy you listened to them. I'm so happy you are so happy. I just knew this was the right move for you. I can feel great things coming for us. I can feel it in my bones. This will be a wild, magical ride." Victoria let go of the embrace and smiled widely.

"It has been a magical ride ever since we heard about the course for the first time." Amber laughed a bit, realizing they had already gone through a lot of ups and downs.

"I still can't believe regular people like us could possibly have a chance to live like this. A few months ago, as I went through my routine, I didn't know any of this was possible, and suddenly, now I have a mission, I have a teacher, I can see spirits, and I can communicate to them," Amber shared, still amazed at how things could change so quickly. "Vic, we can help people—like, for real. We have the capacity to influence the world around us, and we don't need to be sacrificing hours under the sun to do it like they say in school."

"What do you mean?" Victoria laughed at Amber's last sentence.

"Well, I have always wanted to help, you know. I've worked with charities and community work to build schools and stuff like that, but it never felt rewarding, not really. This, on the other hand, feels incredible. People really open up to you; they trust you with their heaviest moments of the past. They feel so much better as they walk out the door and miracles began to happen in their lives. I'm in love with this path." Amber continued as she lay on her bed facing the ceiling with her hands under her head.

"Yeah, I know what you mean. I feel way more connected to people now. It is beautiful to see how the problems the patients share are usually things I have lived as well, even sometimes stuff I'm dealing with at that particular moment." Victoria opened her bedsheets, all ready to get herself into bed.

"My whole life I have wondered what my purpose here was, and now I finally understand. I feel like I'm remembering all I felt I had forgotten. It is such an indescribable feeling. It just feels so ... familiar. I felt completely comfortable getting that energy out of Greta." Amber shared in disbelief.

"Oh, you were paired up with Greta?" Victoria laughed, mocking her apparent misfortune.

"Don't be mean," Amber laughed. "I also feel like such an idiot for considering quitting," she admitted.

Victoria laughed, enjoying every second of what she was about to say. "I told you so!" she indulged.

"Good night," Amber whispered abruptly and continued to laugh as she stared at the ceiling for a few more minutes.

"Night, night." Victoria smiled and turned in her bed, facing the wall behind her, ready to sleep.

Amber took various deep breaths filled with satisfaction and gratitude. Then she managed to pull her red leather journal out of her tightly packed bag. She wrote …

> I mean … I have never felt this amazing in my entire life. I don't know if it is because Greta took that dense energy out of me, because I managed to face my fear successfully, or because I'm so excited for all that comes next. What a beautiful life I'm living right now. I feel like lifetimes of bitterness are beginning to dissolve, and light is beginning to flow into me again. I feel at home. These ladies understand me, they believe in the same things I believe in, and I finally feel like I'm genuinely a part of something. I can't wait to graduate and be able to help others, share these teachings one day, and feel like my time here on Earth is worthwhile. I can't wait to feel innocent again, refreshed, and loved

by all there is. Thank you, Universe. Thank you, God. Thank you, life! Words will never suffice.

Right then and there, Amber opened to the full commitment shamanism requires. Her senses where heightened, and the happiness she felt was palpable. She committed to live from that moment on in service to others. She realized her time on Earth was limited, and she wanted to change it for the better. She felt inspired to truly impact people around her through whichever form they allowed. She understood a simple smile, a kind gesture, or a full-blown intervention could all change the lives of people who were willing to open their hearts to love.

Pain was familiar to her. She thought she knew pain perfectly, but the months ahead would prove otherwise. She still had a lot to learn.

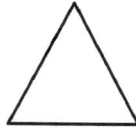

CHAPTER 21

"She shouldn't be allowed in this course. She's like sixteen," Greta insisted to her friend Simone in the parking area of the house. She wasn't whispering; instead, she was bickering with her.

"She's not sixteen. She's twenty-two, Greta. Come on," Simone barked back. "What's your problem?"

"I just feel like she's not mature enough to receive these teachings. What if she were to tell her little friends all about these ancient teachings? Do you know what consequences that can have? That girl Victoria is too young too. Only very responsible, elder people should be able to receive these lessons to ensure they would honor them truly. I personally think it's a way of ensuring the impeccability behind the passing on of this wisdom. Down the road, some of these women will be guided into teaching this very course. How can she possibly understand the responsibility of that at her age?" Greta insisted.

"Look, age is just a number in this lifetime. If she was brought here, it's because she has the same capacity to integrate it that you have, Greta—even at twenty-two. She managed to do the therapy perfectly when, at the same time, your ego got in your way. No one is more or less than anybody else. Focus on your own path, focus on doing everything as impeccably as you can possibly do things, and you will succeed. You don't need to put others down to appear more successful," Simone explained to her longtime friend compassionately, yet authoritatively.

"That is not what I am doing, Simone. Give me some credit. I have been through countless spiritual paths. You know me. You know I am self-aware. I just seriously believe this will harm the quality of how shamanism is expressed in the world after this course ends. She will mess up. I can feel it."

"It also seems like you are waiting for it, Greta." Simone looked at her suspiciously. "You have a lot of work to do. Ask yourself what your fixation with these girls is. Work on it."

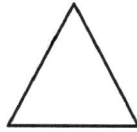

CHAPTER 22

No amount of exhaustion got in the way of Amber's profound sense of completion. She felt elated and honored to be capable of receiving these lessons, techniques, and opportunities. She became very loyal to Simone as time went by. She honored her profoundly as her teacher, her friend, and her role model.

Amber had always had issues with authority. Her capacity of discernment, common sense, and wisdom had been developing for years, and she felt no obligation to listen to authority figures she didn't agree with. Amber was a bit rebellious. But Simone seemed different from the authority figures who had previously tried to impose their beliefs on Amber. Everything Simone shared resonated deeply within Amber's heart. Amber had her head placed properly and firmly on her shoulders, and very few opinions could move her will.

The group still had two more days to go, and these days revolved around the teachings shared earlier. They learned numerous ways to identify symptoms, causes, and roots of different issues within patients. They became wiser by the minute as they were taught to develop self-mastery of their every thought. They experienced late nights under the stars, communicating with different spirits in search of ancient wisdom and answers for their lives. They used drums, crystals, feathers, smoke, and meditation to deepen their altered states of consciousness. They experienced early mornings of exhaustion and incessant crying as they continued to heal the wounds held within the layers of their pasts. They felt the most profound compassion as they saw their newfound friends struggle to heal, learn, and continue to expose their shadows. They felt supported every time they each faced their demons and began to rely on the profound love that was offered to them by the members of the group.

They went through three more rites of passage from the Munay-Ki transmissions. From inside of their energy fields, they received bands of protection that would make negative energies bounce from them without penetrating their systems. They received archetypical forces within each of the energy centers in their bodies, called chakras, which would allow them to have a deeper understanding of what they lived. The last one of the rites they went through was the Seer's Rite, in which a pathway was created between the third eye, brain, and heart that would allow them to begin perceiving the world of invisible energies around them. Their bodies shed years and years of pain in all its manifestations.

They closed the second course feeling renewed

and madly devoted to their spiritual paths. Their lives changed dramatically, and they were beginning to evolve out of what used to be their reality and into a much loving, beautiful, and heartfelt life. Simone shared with the women briefly how they needed to continue doing the extraction therapies as homework among many other assignments, which included reading books, continuing their daily meditation practice, and continuing to develop their intuitive abilities.

They also covered briefly how the third course was the one that would allow them to begin seeing the real beauty of life. They would begin to take flight into the most miraculous aspects of this world, where nothing was out of their league. They would learn how there was nothing they couldn't achieve, do, or be. They would learn how they could manifest anything they wished for into existence, easily.

Amber felt like her whole personality had shifted. She felt vibrant. Nothing could possibly bother her anymore. Ordinary problems seemed so empty to her after experiencing the depths of the human spirit. She embodied peace and serenity in every breath. After the retreat was over, her life continued to change. She felt so empowered knowing her deepest fears had nothing on her anymore. Every aspect of her life, which was previously holding her back, disappeared or drifted. She never again had a nightmare. Her relationships improved, she met interesting people who shared her same beliefs, and she received innumerable blessings in her career path.

Everything seemed to begin flowing effortlessly, and

she couldn't help comparing it to a deal with God. She had heard that there were some powerful figures in the world who had made deals with the devil to receive the power and world leader status. She felt she had done the same thing but with God instead. She felt like ever since the moment she decided to devote her life to the service of her patients, everything was given to her. Things began to unfold naturally, allowing incredible possibilities into her life without requiring from her any more effort than it was to just show up.

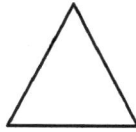

CHAPTER 23

Amber scribbled into her red leather journal one evening, observing the sunset from her city apartment.

When one experiences the depth of true pain, it can be difficult to even attempt to consider healing. When our lives revolve around running away from what has become our cross, we are happy to just be able to function. True pain is silent. True pain breaks you. It breaks a part of you that you didn't know could be broken. True pain allows you to become humble. It makes you a better person as it simultaneously pushes everything you could possibly want away. When we are broken, we remain broken until we accomplish the immeasurable task of asking for help. When we ask for help, we are exposed. We are seen, and that hurts. When we ask for help, we open the door to disappointment. *What if it doesn't work? What if I can't ever feel whole again? Could I live with that? How can I continue to live?*

Real compassion comes in when we realize everyone we see is dealing with inner struggles we know nothing about. Real compassion appears when we can see behind the hurtful words, behind the insults, and into that wounded child who is inside the person attempting to hurt us. That child within you needs a hug. That child needs to be pulled out of the shadows and spider webs of deception and into a ray of warm sunshine. That child has grown tired of living in the dungeon of your subconscious mind. He needs you to let some light in and just give him a hug—a hug that lasts for enough time for him to be rescued by you, so you can be rescued by yourself.

We are all hurting in one way or another either silently or loudly. We are all one, and everything you are dealing with, I have experienced myself. Everything I have had trouble with will creep into your experience as well. We are mirrors. We are all an intertwined part of a dream that we are all simultaneously creating. To heal you, means to heal me. To heal myself, I need to heal you. To understand what I need to work on, I need to stop working on it and instead listen to you. You are me in a way I can't see myself.

Coming close to the idea of opening that box in which everything is cleverly hidden begins to create resistance—a form of resistance you can only identify after countless nights of wondering what's wrong with you. Things begin to awaken within you, and you'll wonder if it is anything else but that—that which you have been refusing to admit or refusing to explore. It feels like a big, grey, safe box locked within chains. It seems so complicated you would rather walk around it than open it. We will always choose to walk around it, but that's not how things change. We know it's just too uncomfortable, too intimidating, too complicated, and way too much work. Sometimes we don't even know where to begin. But as soon as we begin wondering, it all begins to unfold.

There's beauty, and there's beauty, but the kind that I feel drawn to is the shine in people's eyes that somehow allows you to feel the beauty of their sacred wounds. Beauty, to me, is the open door, regardless of what we may find inside. Having the door to our hearts open is just the most beautiful thing in the world. Observing someone's soul and feeling it being pure gives you a form of inspiration that bounces around in your head inevitably. Those people who, regardless of their wounds, allow themselves to be completely transparent and open in their hearts are the ones worth listening to—those who put it all out there knowing the risk of being hurt but sleeping peacefully at night knowing it will be the way it's meant to. Find those people. Lean on them.

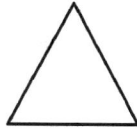

CHAPTER 24

"**S**oul retrieval is the jewel of shamanism, I believe." Simone had a bite of her organic leafy green salad. "Helping spirits are generous once you show them you are showing up to help another human being. They will show you everything you need to know, including memories and information from the patient's past to share with the patient.

"So, how does it work?" Amber asked as she continued to eat her meal as well.

"It's like a journey or guided meditation. You go on a journey to retrieve a missing piece of the person's soul—one that was scared off by trauma, emotional pain, accidents, or surgeries." Simone shared generously with Amber as they had lunch in the usual hotel they had gotten used to meeting at once every few weeks.

Simone had found Amber to be a great source of advice for her as well. Amber was hungry for a deeper understanding of basically anything Simone would be willing to share with her. Every time they met, Amber felt connected again to whatever it was that made her feel whole. The whole course brought that energy toward her in different forms or variations. She would feel whole when exposed to the ladies, the healing therapies, or the teachings.

"So, if that's at the third retreat, what's at the fourth one?" Amber took a sip of her watermelon juice.

"At the forth one, you will all be graduating hopefully. You will receive the Star Keeper's Rite and the Earth Keeper's Rite among tons of new techniques, methods, and insights. You will just reach a new height. You will remember your connection to all there is, and that will probably have its consequences in your life as well. You will grasp the concept of 'we are all one' in a way that will be undeniable to you.

"Graduating is the biggest honor you will probably experience in this lifetime. Naturally, there will be forces trying to stop that. You will be tested incessantly until proven worthy of graduation. I like to think it's not that way, but through the years, I have found that not everybody is cut out for the gig. Remember the Wheel of Medicine Course can often feel like an obstacle race instead of a course. When you graduate, the course will be over, yet it will open the door for a lifetime of service. That's where the real work begins," Simone shared, having a wonderful time with her apprentice.

"Ah!" Amber sighed in amusement. "I can't wait. I never thought being a healer was my thing. I had no idea I would enjoy it, let alone be good at it. They are moments to connect to the divine and become transparent. It's like I return to source, and I have permission to leave the human version of me outside the room for a bit. It's very relieving."

"Yeah, I know what you mean. Well, it is your mission. That's why it feels so good," Simone explained. "You have found your mission at such a young age," she whispered nostalgically. "You have a lot of time ahead of you to develop your gifts, to share them, and to have such a profound impact. Your journey will be beautiful to watch. Remember that when you are struggling with the tests the Universe will place in your path. Remember that every single test is just an opportunity the Universe is giving you to grow and evolve," Simone reminded her.

"When you say tests, what do you mean?" Amber asked curiously.

"Well, like the hauntings. Those were clearly tests for you to overcome your fears. You learned a lot by overcoming those fears, and now you truly understand what it means to be empowered. The second retreat was the one dedicated to facing our fears. Everybody was tested in different ways, addressing their own personal fears," Simone explained.

"I felt like I was temporarily crazy. Looking back, I feel ridiculous to have experienced those fears and can't even relate to them," Amber shared, looking at Simone directly.

"Everything dissolves once you face it—problems, fears, and nervousness. Shed some light on them, and they will immediately dissolve." Simone crossed her arms over her chest.

△

CHAPTER 25

After half a year of deep spiritual purification, it was time to begin having some fun. During the first and second retreats, the women had focused on reclaiming their lost energy, traveling back to heal every moment of pain from this and past lifetimes, and learning to get themselves into the best shape possible, energetically speaking. It had been tough, but it had also been beautiful and sacred. Now it was time for the third retreat—the direction of the north.

The Hummingbird Medicine would teach them how to enjoy life intensely and how to find profound gratitude within themselves to honor everything that had lived up to that point. After the necessary skin was shredded, metaphorically, during the first retreat, they had become strong enough to face their deepest fears at the second retreat. It was time now for each of them to learn how to co-create the life of her dreams. They would begin to learn how to manifest blessings, attract opportunities, and begin to design their lives with the help of the Universe, God, and the angels.

All the participants had lived through countless tests at this point, and they had all developed a sense of detachment from any kind of physical reality. They knew anything could be taken from them at any moment, but that wasn't a problem because happiness was already within. Their sense of security began to appear in their souls instead of their lives. Like birds, they began trusting their wings more than the branches below them.

This time, the procedure to learn was soul retrieval, which would bring back into each of them lost parts of her essential energy and life force. Each woman would become whole again, bringing back every single piece of her soul lost during her life due to disappointments, emotional trauma, difficult situations, or surgeries.

The challenging part of the course was over. It was time to enjoy pure bliss and connection to divine energies. They had earned the right to learn how to make their lives become pure magic on daily basis. They had earned the right to receive all they had ever dreamed of—for the highest good of all involved, that is.

CHAPTER 26

"On the journey, I saw, through my mind's eye, a big car crash. I saw a small white car being completely flipped upside down on the side of a highway. The concrete color was a dark grey, and there were mountains in the background. Golden dry grass peacefully swayed in the wind. The car had flipped down and away from the highway over a small hill. There was fire. I saw you, and you were bleeding, but you were okay. I could tell it had somehow been your fault— the accident. Or maybe you felt that way. I could feel a lot of guilt and panic coming from you. Master Jesus was guiding me through the scene, and he told me you were with a girlfriend in the car. You both made it. He explained to me you felt a lot of guilt, and he wanted to let you know that she forgives you completely. She has moved on, and you need to forgive yourself as well, he said. He wants you to understand that nothing happens by mistake and that, even if you feel like you have moved on, there's some energy in there that still needs to be released." Amber shared slowly as she kneeled next to Marie.

"A fragment of your soul was scared off in that moment due to the intense shock of the crash. That energy and essence was ready to come back to you, so I brought it back and placed it inside your heart chakra, as Master Jesus guided me to. It was so intense. I can't explain the vividness of the vision shown to me." Amber spoke compassionately to Marie, who was still lying down on the grass, lingering on every word Amber shared.

So, that's what a soul retrieval feels like, huh? Amber thought.

Marie's blue eyes watered naturally, and she began to shift her position to sit down. She leaned toward Amber, reaching for a hug with a smile drawn upon her closed lips. They hugged for a while, feeling completely relaxed and connected by such an intense level of magic. Their energies had drifted so much from the beginning of the year till this moment that they were no longer surprised or shocked with the intensity of each exercise. Instead, exercises would reassure them the expected magic that was possible through shamanism. The beauty had become a natural state of living for them.

"So, Marie, was the vision accurate?" Amber let go of the embrace and placed her hand over Marie's knee. They were kneeling across from each other on the wet grass.

"Yes, completely." Marie wiped her tears away and smiled. "I was in my twenties, traveling through South America. My friend was driving, and I don't remember

127

perfectly, but something happened. It had something to do with a big truck coming at us. Instinctively, I reached for the steering wheel violently. We pulled it in different directions, and we wound up flipped over on the side of the road. I remember blood, and I still have the scars on different parts of my body. See?" Marie showed Amber a three-inch scar on her forearm and explained to her there were many more also.

"We both got hurt. Nothing mayor, but we can't say we walked out of it without a scratch. I always felt so guilty. It's true. I never really addressed or healed that situation. I didn't know how back then. My friend and I grew apart, and I always wondered how my life would be different if she hadn't made it." Marie's eyes began to water again as she moved her long grey hair out of the way.

"But she did make it. It is in the past now, and I received the message that she has completely forgiven you. It is time for you to do the same for yourself." Amber continued to touch Marie's knee, showing her support and smiling gently, letting her know it was all okay.

"You are right. That was intense. You received so many details. It's very impressive how the soul retrievals will allow you to have really clear visions." Marie noted.

"It is. Sometimes when I meditate, I receive symbols, messages, and images. But this felt like I was there—like I had traveled back in time. It was as if Master Jesus was guiding me, and we walked around the area, looking at the car wreck. He explained to me everything I needed to know," Amber shared, realizing it was, indeed, very intense.

"You work a lot with Jesus, don't you?" Marie asked her shyly.

"I mean, I love Jesus … always have. My family raised me to be a Catholic, and now I accept guidance and love from all sorts of helping spirits, but he always seems to be around me. It makes me really happy to work with him, and I feel safe every time," Amber admitted. "He's, after all, known as the most powerful metaphysical master of all time."

"Yeah, it's pleasant to see how much he guides you. I wonder who will be guiding me when I do the soul retrieval on you." Marie shifted the focus from herself onto Amber, which reminded her remember it was her turn now as she smiled mysteriously.

Amber laid down with her back on the grass. She saw the clear sky above her and felt grateful to be supported by Mother Earth in that way. She realized how everything felt easy. Her capacity to appreciate life had increased dramatically, and now even the sound of a little bird beside her would fill up her soul with joy. Marie sat down crossed-legged next to her patient with her journal in hand, reviewing every step of the soul retrieval procedure before beginning. Amber closed her eyes and breathed deeply. She allowed her mind to drift as Marie placed her hand over Amber's forearm to remain connected during the procedure.

In Marie's mind, she began to imagine the path she had grown so familiar with, going into the underworld. She saw herself walking on a beautiful mountain and then entering a small, dark cave on the side of it. She walked through the cave and over to what seemed like a gateway leading up to a beautiful forest. There were three steps she had to go down to enter. She had used this path countless times for many of the meditations, journeys, procedures, and readings. She felt at home on this path.

For the soul retrieval, however, she needed to go even deeper into that realm. Using specific directions, she would reach Huascar, the guardian of the Underworld. He has also been referred to as the guardian of the subconscious mind. Once she reached what seemed like beautiful house with gardens and trees everywhere, she found her way to a door, which she figured was the door that Huascar, the guardian, would answer. This was all going on in her mind—a journey she was going through with her eyes closed as she sat crossed-legged next to Amber, who was lying down on the grass.

Marie gently knocked on the door, and a small, indigenous man opened the door. He was presented to her as a man who could have been sixty years old. His skin was leathery and wrinkly. He's eyes were kind, dark, and small. As he looked up at her, he smiled. He was wearing a simple white shirt and dark pants. He took a step out of the doorway. He was barefoot, and his feet seemed as dusty as the ground beneath them.

"Welcome," he said kindly.

"It's an honor, Lord Huascar. I'm very happy to meet you. I'm here on behalf of Amber Marie Macintosh. She has given me permission to come here and ask you to help me retrieve a fragment of her soul she has previously lost. I would love your guidance and support. This is my first time doing this," she said politely.

"Absolutely. Follow me," he said.

Immediately she felt a sense of relief. Apparently, sometimes he told practitioners that it was not the right time to do this on behalf of the patient. If he said the patient was not ready, Marie would have needed to listen and journey all the way back with no success.

In shamanism, relationships are formed with a lot of different guardians, spirits, and guides. They can be formed into deep relationships of love and trust, or just be accessed in order to receive information on behalf of patients. This doesn't necessarily influence the practitioner's spiritual beliefs. Practitioners acknowledge the existence and presence of these beings and respectfully communicate with them when necessary.

Marie was guided to walk into what seemed like a long, warm hallway with four doors on the left side. Although this was how the place looked to Marie in her mind, all practitioners would see it differently, based on their own impressions and preferences. She saw the doors, which were separated from each other by about three meters. The doors where white, and there were decorative plants placed on the floor to the right of each door. There wasn't really anything else in that space besides the doors and plants. Huascar guided her to stand outside of the first white door.

"In here you will peek at the moment in which the wound was formed. You will see with as many details as you allow the exact moment in which the soul fragment left the patient's body. Trust fully in everything you perceive. I will be serving as your guide today. Remember, the first things that pop into your mind are your answers. Trust that they are accurate. Try to just be an observer of it all, and avoid your personal thoughts from interfering," he reminded her.

"Thank you so much!" Marie said to him genuinely as she began to open the door.

Once she stepped inside the room, she noticed a tiny white dog barking at her. She observed him for a little bit and then proceeded to enter the space, looking for any representation of Amber. Then, at a distance, she saw what looked like eight-year-old Amber. Marie approached her and asked her what she was doing there. The little girl replied that the white dog was her pet, and she mentioned how her mother decided to take him away and put him to sleep without letting her say good-bye to him. The little girl began to cry as Marie tried to convince her to go with her, back into "adult Amber's" life.

During soul retrievals, the practitioner is expected to convince that frightened part of the patient's soul, which is usually represented by the image of a younger version of the patient, to come back with them and be retrieved on behalf of the patient's well-being. Sometimes the fragments willingly accept to come back to complete the previously fragmented soul, but other times they need convincing. To do so, the practitioner will sometimes need to engage in negotiation with the soul fragment in a language it would understand, varying from age to age, in order to convince it to come back.

The sudden change in vibration from high to low when a person is presented with a moment of emotional shock makes the essential soul energy held inside fragmented. A fragment often escapes, taking away with it some of the pain and shock. If patients are addicted to destructive patterns, whether they are substances, relationships, or habits, those fragments that have escaped will be harder to retrieve and bring back. If the soul fragment can perceive that it will be brought back into an unhealthy scenario, it will usually try its best to resist the soul retrieval. That energy doesn't want to be exposed to anything that could possibly scare it off again.

Marie continued with the process, going through all the steps and stages of it until she reached the point when she was ready to bring back that energy into Amber's being. As she came back from her journey, she blew this energy into Amber's heart chakra, and they both remained silent for a bit.

Amber could feel the energy coming back into her. She felt immediately clearer in her mind, and she could tell it worked. Thanks to Marie, Amber was beginning to become whole again. She felt the effects on herself after a few days, feeling cheerful, confident, empowered, and natural within her own skin.

CHAPTER 27

The sound of the rattles seemed louder than ever, the nausea in her body began to expand, and a feeling of quiet desperation began to creep in within Amber's body. After hours of ritual, the images in her eyes began to dissolve into hazy shadows and intense colors that moved to the beat of the drums. Her head was pounding as she drifted further and further into trance. The sounds began to be too loud for her to comfortably tolerate, and she would jump on her seat, trying to stay awake. Amber's long white sundress had been stained by a drop of blood coming from her fingertips. Her wavy brown hair was decorated with a crown of pink and white flowers, making her look like the goddess she was always meant to be.

Simone's body was trembling slowly as she allowed the energy of an indigenous elder to take over her body and perform the ritual. Her face morphed and showed the muscle tics that elder must have had back when he lived. Her face began to look ancient, and the skin on her face seemed to hang, making her look at least twenty years older than she was. As she hunched over, wearing a thick, dark throw over her shoulders, she went through different movements and blessings for each one of the ladies who, one by one, came to sit on the floor in front of her, just like at the previous rituals. Beside Simone there was a big chunk of black tourmaline crystal placed on the floor—a great tool to ward off evil spirits.

Amber was the first one to receive the vibrational frequency of angels and archangels within her body. The new high vibrational energy within her struggled to settle within her dense physical reality. The nausea and headache began to feel unbearable, but she was happy she had graduated. She stared aimlessly at the floor in front of her when she was suddenly interrupted by what seemed like a lighting strike directly to her heart. Instinctively, she looked back to Simone, trying to grasp some air again, and found that she was staring directly into her eyes, which crept Amber out immediately. The look in Simone's eyes left Amber petrified, and she could feel an electrical current passing through her skin at what seemed like the speed of light. She couldn't help trembling herself, as goose bumps ran up and down her arms, and the knot she felt in her stomach began to expand to her heart area as well.

Simone continued with the ritual, leaving Amber completely confused and moved by what had just happened.

Did Simone do that? Did the elder do that? Amber

thought to herself. *But why? Are they trying to keep me awake?*

The speed of the drumming increased, and so did her sense of weakness. After a few short moments, which felt like hours to Amber, the drums and the rattles controlled by the ladies from the group came to an abrupt stop. The scent of tobacco began to fill the space with no one lighting any tobacco leaves, and the indigenous elder made his exit. Simone's body dropped to the floor, motionless.

"Don't trust anyone blindly, Amber, not even Simone." A masculine voice spoke into her mind, one that Amber could barely address due to what had just happened to Simone.

After seeing Simone's body collapse, their initial reaction was to stand up alarmed and start approaching her, but before anyone did, Greta signaled them to stay put. Assuring them with her eyes, they could see Simone just needed a minute.

CHAPTER 28

The impossibly hard task of surviving the last retreat was rewarded by a hot shower at four thirty in the morning, right before heading back to the city later that day. Amber's hair smelled like bonfire smoke mixed with lavender oil. Her skin felt sweaty, her body was completely rundown, and her mind was finally relieved. The impossible was accomplished. She could rest peacefully for a few hours, and for her, that was the best graduation present. As she washed her body, she realized she could barely hold any thoughts in her mind. She continued to feel nauseous, and her headache began to feel more like a migraine. She had no idea graduation would feel like this.

She came back to the dorm room where she was staying, this time with most the ladies. She got into her bed, hoping to recover or at least pass out. The ritual had clearly created a different reaction in all the other students. They were screaming, laughing, joking, and acting out in celebration. Every sound penetrated Amber's mind, increasing the pain exponentially. She covered her head with a pillow, trying to ignore the noise. It was pointless as she realized the loudest and most obnoxious one of all was Simone. She began to pay attention to what she was saying, impressed to be faced with such a complete opposite version of the teacher she thought she knew.

After a full year shared, Simone had always been kind, funny, and gracious. Suddenly, this completely new person rose from within her. Her comments seemed abusive, her sense of humor was inappropriate, and her hope seemed to be to just keep them awake. Many of the girls were as tired as Amber was, trying to sleep and telling Simone and the other ladies to drop it. But they would instead throw pillows at them, insisting it was time to celebrate. The pain in Amber's head was so intense that her eyes started to water. She felt completely hopeless and disappointed to realize that even after all the effort she'd made, she wouldn't be able to rest at all.

With the little energy she had left, she turned around and told them all she was feeling awful and that she really needed to rest. Simone, who up to this point had been so supportive and understanding, mocked her and began to ridicule her. The confusion that began to rise within Amber had no way of being described as she struggled to see straight in the first place. She was in no capacity to translate what was going on, so she just grabbed her pillow and headed for the bathroom. She locked the door in desperation, listening to the laughter.

She lay on the bathroom floor, finally in a bit of quiet, and allowed her heavy eyes to get some rest.

After a few minutes, Simone came rushing to knock on the bathroom door.

"Are you crying?" Simone asked loudly with the seeming intention of having the others listen.

"Go away! I just need to rest, Simone. Come on," Amber replied, incredibly annoyed.

She had no energy left to fight. She had no energy to string her thoughts together appropriately, let alone interact with the teacher she looked up to. She couldn't afford to wonder what had happened to the teacher she supposedly knew. She just needed some time and space.

"I really need the bathroom!" Simone continued, clearly meaning to continue her behavior.

Amber walked out the bathroom, and as she looked at Simone briefly, the same feeling of disgust she felt on the first rite began to creep in within her. Amber began to feel like an old elder again, looking at a clueless apprentice with pity. She was surprised to remember that she had already felt that way once toward Simone with no apparent reason at the beginning of it all. That moment at the beginning of the course began to make sense now more than ever.

Simone smiled like a four-year-old girl as she closed the door to use the bathroom, and Amber headed for the house door to leave. Her car was outside, and she figured she could pass out in there till the morning. As she realized the door was locked, she gave up in exhaustion and sat on the floor next to the door. Some of the ladies came in to meet her and began to finally understand how awful she had been feeling for the past couple of hours. They were worried and brought their healing tools with the best of intentions to help her.

"How can you all possibly be acting like this?" Amber said calmly with rage in her voice. "There's an empty living room here. Why aren't you choosing to celebrate there instead of in the bedroom where clearly I am not the only one whose body is breaking down?"

The ladies gave her reason and allowed her to get back to her bed. The level of rage she was feeling made her shake uncontrollably, as her body had clearly taken a turn for the worse after the graduation ritual. The new energies within her system began to alter the state of every single layer of her being, and she was feeling every minute of it. Some of the other ladies seemed to be sleeping, and Amber felt happy to see they had escaped the discomfort she had somehow fallen into.

As Amber got ready to finally get some rest, Greta was the last one to walk out the door as she whispered arrogantly, to the other ladies. "It's okay. Some people can't handle rituals as well as we can."

Greta closed the door behind her, and Amber felt enraged. She remained in such an awe that everything they had been integrating, learning, and experiencing as far as being nice, polite, respectful, and loving had been thrown out the window to the expense of some old lady hangout. What you claim to have learned well enough to earn a graduation of this kind shouldn't have an on-and-off switch. Out of all the possible scenarios she expected to experience for graduation, this was not one of them. She couldn't craft one to be more disappointing if she tried.

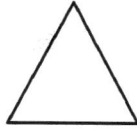

CHAPTER 29

"I was just disappointed. I expected the support and care of you all. I needed help, but instead I got ridiculed by those I thought would protect me if necessary. It just hurts, I guess. Especially with the way I'm feeling, everything irritates me, and the intensity of everything increases," Amber explained to Simone as she lay on the cold grass at five o'clock in the morning.

Birds were chirping, and Simone seemed pissed. She cleared some energy from Amber's mind, trying to ease her discomfort. Simone didn't say a word, and Amber felt uncomfortable to receive her assistance under such circumstances.

"Greta said there are people who don't react well to rituals—not as well as others at least. Did I do something wrong that might have made me feel this way?" Amber continued, ignoring Simone's cold and empty look.

"What Greta said is true, but what I believe is that some of us open up to receive way more energy than others. You opened up completely. It's a good thing. Your body just needs to overcome the adjustments, which will probably be intense," Simone replied gently, seeming more like the teacher Amber knew and loved.

They remained silent while the coolness of the morning refreshed their skin and the sun slowly began to appear. Amber felt worried. She was worried about herself, about her body, and, most importantly, about that completely new side she had seen Simone expose. It was interesting to her, to say the least, to see how someone's entire personality could shift before her eyes in a split second. Amber had a hard time trusting others in the first place, so this naturally spiked her curiosity.

The journey had been magical, and the whole year was a sacred time of expansion for her. It was strange to have it end with a weird taste to it. She hoped that when she felt better, all those emotions would be released, and she could enter a state of gratitude and honor again. No matter how hard she tried during the following hours, she couldn't shake off the masculine voice that had whispered into her mind: "Don't trust anyone blindly, not even Simone."

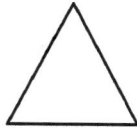

CHAPTER 30

Amber's life felt so different. For the following three days after graduation, she would see people's colorful auras dancing around them at the supermarket, she would accidentally hear people's thoughts at the movies, and she would see picture-perfect images of the future in her dreams, only to have them appear in her life a few days later. She could see what seemed to be fairies, lights, and shadows everywhere.

The world looked different, and she felt insignificant and almighty at the same time. She wondered if she would see the world that way forever. She worried something had just opened up within her and that the world would look this way forever. It was a bit much. She imagined hallucinogenic drugs likely caused a similar high to the one she was feeling.

She began to feel very detached from her human reality as she held a sense of knowingness that assured her that no matter what happened next in her path, it would be a test for which she would come out of victorious. Every experience a person lives through can either become a lesson or a wound. The person gets to choose how involved he or she wants to be, how much power to give to any situation and how long to indulge in recovering from it. Sometimes, it takes time to heal—yes. Sometimes people choose for it to take way longer that it needs to.

Over time, Amber's guides became her teachers, and Simone became an alley on her journey. The small incidents were kept behind as they deepened their relationship as peers, discussing projects and future retreats to help those around them. Amber naturally began having an impact on her generation, which hadn't received many of these insights, especially from someone their same age. Amber's mission was unfolding before her, and the choices the Universe made on her behalf were better than what she could've hoped for.

The months went by, and the universal forces seemed to align everything for her. The studio she was working in was planning to close its doors for good, so she volunteered to keep it, and the owner gave it to her— just like that. She began hosting small meditations and offering her therapies. That, as it was, was a dream come true. Then her patient list began to expand, and she even had people on a waiting list for weeks. She felt so blessed to be able to receive so many patients and have such a profound impact in such a short amount of time.

She felt blessed and accomplished. She felt like her entire life was beginning to shape up in ways she would have never dreamed of. The gratitude in her heart was only trumped by her thirst for life. She realized there were no limits whatsoever to what anyone can manifest into reality, so she decided to go all the way and manifest her dreams right then and there.

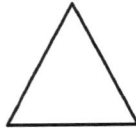

CHAPTER 31

"Hey, Vic, what's up?" Amber answered the phone enthusiastically as she drove back home.

"Hey, doll. I just came out of therapy with Simone." Victoria sounded confused.

"Yeah? Cool. How do you feel?" Amber asked her, noticing the tone of her voice.

"What happened between you two?" Victoria continued.

"What do you mean?"

"Well, I was meeting her up at nine o'clock this morning, and she was enraged, talking about how you had betrayed the medicine and speaking really poorly about you for about two hours—which was completely wasting my time, by the way. And then we started the therapy. It was so bizarre and uncomfortable. She knows I'm your friend. Why on earth would she speak to me about you like that?" Victoria explained, sounding annoyed.

"I have no idea what you are talking about." Amber's expression changed completely. "That I betrayed the medicine? How on earth could I have betrayed the medicine? I'm super careful during each therapy I do. I haven't done any mistakes that I know of. What could she possibly mean?" Amber's forehead tightened deeper into tension.

"Yeah, I don't know, but she was pissed. She even said she would take your mesa away." Vic sounded worried as she spoke those words.

"I don't understand. Everything is flowing perfectly. If I had indeed betrayed the medicine, one of my guides would have said something. It would have been reflected somehow. I would know if I had messed up," Amber answered, confused.

"That's what I thought. Look, I know you. I'm sure if you made a mistake, you will be able to fix it. Plus, honestly, it sounded to me like she was jealous," Victoria admitted.

"I can't imagine that being the case. What could she possibly be jealous about? She's our teacher. She taught us all of these principles. She has more self-control than that." Amber defended her lightly as she continued to wonder. "Well, I'll call her. I'll fix this."

Amber's stomach sank into a void as she hung up the phone. She had no idea what was going on. Amber's immediate reaction was to call Simone, who didn't answer. She left a message for her. In the meantime, she retraced every step from everything she had done recently—every recent therapy, every recent conversation with a patient, every meditation—and she couldn't find anything that she was aware would "betray shamanic medicine." On the contrary, Amber was proud by how truthful her intentions really were. She did nothing without the patient's highest interest in mind. She retraced every single piece of advice offered to her countless patients as follow-up for their therapies, and she couldn't find any recklessness anywhere.

A few days went by, and Amber felt like she was driving herself crazy. She connected to her guides several times, and they all assured she had nothing to worry about.

Her spirit guide, the wolf, told her: "Your physical life reflects your inner state. If your life is being filled with opportunities, dreams coming true, and tons of patients to help, you are doing what you need to be doing. All is well. All is well. Trust yourself."

Easier said than done. This was messing with her head—big time. The biggest honor she had ever experienced was going through this process and being worthy of calling herself a pure channel. If that was taken away from her, everything around her would begin to crumble. If Simone took away her mesa, she would, technically, take away her possibility to heal others. Why would she possibly want to do that, considering that Amber was helping so many people? If both of their goals were to help the world around them and help awaken the community in which they were both living, what would the benefit be?

Amber couldn't stop thinking about it. She felt how her dream life began to be tainted by worry and confusion.

She couldn't understand why Simone wouldn't answer her or confront the situation.

Amber began to feel how her reality would soon take a turn in a direction she might not like. She felt like her whole system had been hacked, and she had allowed it.

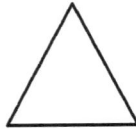

CHAPTER 32

" Check your email inbox," was the only message Simone wrote to Amber.

As Amber felt a sense of relief from finally hearing from her, she felt dread to open that email. As she looked for her laptop, Amber couldn't help but wonder why she would have such a serious conversation over email instead of in person. She had the same exact feeling she had after graduation.

Where do the principles go when it's the time to use them? she thought. Something like this seemed important enough to address it honorably, not comfortably.

When she managed to open her laptop, she found that Simone had written about two pages filled with hateful assumptions and accusations about her. Amber read the email about four times, trying to place herself in Simone's shoes. The feeling of being overwhelmed took over, and Amber slammed her laptop shut again, enraged.

Amber went for a walk without responding. The hurtful words Simone had written bounced around her head as she failed to comprehend everything even after a few hours of contemplation. She felt pain in her heart for having somehow disappointed her teacher, but she felt rage in her being as she knew she had done nothing to be punished for. The confusion was uncomfortable to hold within her body, but she had a clear conscience that any and every decision she'd made so far had been completely fuelled by her intention to serve the world around her, her patients, and future ones. The accusations were based on assumptions, and none of it was reality. Simone had assumed false scenarios of what she thought Amber was planning to do and immediately reacted boldly toward her without checking if what she thought was happening was, indeed, happening.

It's funny how a person may understand, believe, and breathe spiritual principles teaching us how to behave consciously, but as soon as that person is presented with an opportunity to use the teachings, it's easy to forget they exist and react aggressively out of fear instead of love. When people face moments of crisis, those are the perfect chances to implement all they have learned. That is the real test, honestly. The challenge is to hold a detached objective perspective while your heart is in pieces. To continue to have unshakeable faith that everything is in divine order, regardless of what you are facing.

Nobody is perfect, and people will be offered a lot of opportunities to practice what they are trying to learn. They will face countless opportunities to develop that loving, detached perspective if they struggle to find it. The effort that's put into acting instead of reacting will define how many opportunities will be given. Opportunities are moments of crisis or difficulty that will attempt to push a person into using the principles being learned.

"Hey, Amber. I wanted to check up on you and see how things unfolded with Simone," Victoria said through the phone while Amber continued trying to strand sentences together in her mind to deliver a response, answering the email to her teacher.

"She sent me a brutal email. You should read it. It's ridiculous." Amber spoke softly.

"What was the problem anyway?" Victoria asked curiously.

"Do you remember how I was planning to put together three-month coaching packages to offer? Well, I decided I would like to include two healing therapies in the package, and apparently that was too much for her to handle." Amber couldn't help giggling as she explained the email to Victoria.

"What do you mean? She has no business telling you what you can and cannot do in your business." Victoria was dead serious as she spoke.

"I know. She isn't even my teacher anymore. We graduated a while ago. You must read this email, man. She sounds insane," Amber admitted, realizing the situation was completely ridiculous.

"I don't understand. When she talked about what happened to me, she seemed hurt and offended. I feared you had seriously fucked up," Victoria admitted.

"She is seriously offended. She said the most hurtful

things. She said all the things she knew would break me. She was seriously throwing low blows at me, like she wanted to hurt the deepest parts of me. I think she did, actually," Amber said, sounding upset again.

"This is crazy," Victoria answered back. "It clearly isn't about the packages you were planning to offer. It must be about something else. Such a big mess cannot be based on such a ridiculously stupid misunderstanding. It's a high school drama all over again. She'll come around; after all, she taught us how to always leave our egos aside and instead open the door for real communication to take place with others."

"Yeah, I think she meant email wars." Amber laughed again in disbelief of the irony.

After their conversation, Amber tried long and hard to meditate, trying to leave her fears and insecurities aside and listen to her spirit guides. Everybody up there assured her she had been guided into every decision she had taken. If Simone had a problem with it, it was her problem really.

Amber asked during meditation if there was any possibility her mesa would be taken from her. They told her that Simone would try to exercise her authority and take away Amber's mesa, but none of them would let her.

It was impossibly hard for Amber to resist the anger building up inside of her chest. How could she take away from everyone Amber was serving? How could she consider taking away Amber's ability to heal others when there were so many people out there needing help? How could Simone forget that all light workers are catering the same cause? They were all working in the same direction. Amber was creating a powerful ripple effect on the community around her, and she was having a big impact.

Maybe that was the problem.

Amber gathered up and opened her laptop again. She wished to hold a state of calm serenity as she wrote, but that was nearly impossible. She tried to be as respectful, objective, and neutral as possible without letting her feelings interfere with what she was writing. She explained her actual plans to Simone, exposing the reasons and intents behind them. She apologized for any confusions, and she went an extra mile to suck up her ego and only write what would benefit them both, leaving behind how irrational she thought she was being. A part of her thought and hoped Simone would just call her and tell her it was all a weird prank, testing her patience. That never happened. Instead, it continued and became an even bigger issue.

Amber thought about growing up when she would have a conversation with her parents and it was as if they were each talking about something completely different than the other? There was no understanding whatsoever on either side of the argument. That's how this felt for Amber.

As she sent the email, she felt refreshed. She felt proud of herself for being the bigger person and allowing what seemed like perfect opportunities to fire back her opinion slide. She allowed a bright smile to be drawn on her face as she completely trusted on her spirit guides' advice. After all, they had never led her astray.

A few minutes of contemplation later, she received

another long, nasty response. She thought to herself, *You have to be kidding me.* During this round, Simone pointed out to Amber how she didn't seem to have understood any of the lessons from the course, how she seemed to have no idea about how the connection with spirit guides worked, and how she continued to dishonor her path by thinking the way she was thinking. Simone mentioned how Amber was making a fool of herself and how she was hurting the medicine.

Amber sighed, realizing there was no way to win. She wondered for a while if these points could be true. Was it possible she had completely misunderstood how things worked? Was it possible she had been hurting the medicine without realizing it? Was it possible she was, indeed, clueless about how shamanism was supposed to be honored? The doubts began, and the fears crept in.

Could she be right? Could my relationships to my spirit guides be somehow influenced by my preferences? Could their advice not be objective? Amber thought to herself sincerely.

In a split second, something broke. Was there any way in which the perfect life Amber was co-creating with the Universe around her had been an illusion? Everything she knew and trusted, everything that was working out so perfectly for her, was doubted by the only person Amber had truly admired in this lifetime. She felt her power diminishing as confusion crept in, and after that moment, nothing felt the same.

"So, did you respond to her?" Victoria asked after listening to Amber's heartbreaking story over tea the following day.

"No. I have no idea what to say." Amber looked troubled.

"So she didn't really understand any of what you explained to her?" Vic asked again.

"No, Vic, she fired back as quickly as possible, trying to prove how right she obviously was." Amber took a bite from her tomato, olive oil, and mozzarella bruschetta at the Italian restaurant, looking as disappointed as ever.

"I don't understand." Victoria looked at her.

Amber shrugged her shoulders, letting her know she didn't understand a thing either.

They continue to speak for a few hours over a delicious meal overlooking the Panama City skyline. It was Friday night, and they were all dressed up. As best friends, they used to share moments like this often. They talked about it for a while, always returning to the same spot of complete and utter confusion. Victoria would insist from time to time that Simone was just jealous for how successful Amber had become as a healer and how many people were seeking her services. Amber chose to refuse that possibility every time, implying that she deserved more credit than that.

Weeks went by, and nothing had been cleared up. Instead, the feelings of doubt and insecurity began to expand within Amber. She began doubting her healing therapies, she began doubting how efficient she had been, and she began doubting everything that had made her so happy and fulfilled at heart up to that point.

Emotions cloud judgment. When a person is triggered by a situation, the individual doesn't see it for what it is. It's seen as what's being experienced in the tormented space within the mind. It was getting in Amber way. Her heart was in pain. The relationship she had developed with Simone was so essential to her at that point, and she really honored it and respected Simone. Amber felt like she still had so much to learn from Simone, but, apparently, the Universe thought otherwise.

She remembered something Simone herself had said during the training: "Teachers are like streetlights. They will light your path from one section of the road to the next, but after that, another streetlight will be the one that provides the light for you. It is the same with teachers. Don't hold on to any teacher. You will discover everything that happens to you will become your teacher."

Amber's life had been dedicated to shamanism for about two years at that point. It had become her world; the group was her group. She had begun to grow attached to their friendships and their support. When she found people who could understand her when she talked about alternate realities, apparitions, rituals, manifestation, and energy work when no one else did, it was easy to get attached because she genuinely liked them.

Marie, the old traveler guru with grey hair, had become a real friend and inspiration for Amber as well, and she finally felt, within the group, like she belonged.

As soon as the email exchange happened, Amber began to feel the energies of the group shift. She began to feel distant and somehow rejected by the group. After a few uncomfortable conversations, she grew to understand none of them respected her the way she thought. They only considered her the young and immature one from the bunch. She was disappointed to see how none of them seemed to take her seriously. None of them seemed interested in knowing her point of view, her plans, or her perspective. Instead, assumptions continued to form to the point that she felt completely alienated from the group. She felt lonely, and it was hard to believe in herself when none of the people she respected seemed to either.

Amber's unhealed wounds were triggered. The thing is, no matter what happens to a person, what makes that event hurt is the level in which the person chooses to engage and invest energy in it. Initially, it can hurt, but whether the person allows it to truly shake her or just sting a bit reflects how much of her power she is giving to that situation. A person who has achieved complete self-mastery won't be emotionally triggered by the events at hand. The reason why a simple misunderstanding shook Amber's world to that extent was proof of how much work she still had to do to achieve self-mastery.

She felt betrayed, hurt, enraged, and sad. She began bouncing from one emotion to the next involuntarily as a habit for days. Naturally, she began to take it a bit easy and took some time off work to heal herself, leaving her patients hanging and waiting for her to be able to help them again. She had no idea that's what was happening, but she felt herself becoming small again.

Victoria remained her helping hand the whole time and always assured her she had never done anything wrong. When a person is amid something, it's not clear to that person what could be done better, what is hurting, or which consequences are being formed by the way he or she is acting. When a turmoil of a pain in the mind is experienced, it's hard to think straight. Now that Amber felt shaken, she focused on functioning instead of thriving. She doubted her every step.

People are on this Earth for evolution and working their way through to ascension. If people truly wish to evolve, they might need to go through situations that will potentially challenge them. At that point, Amber couldn't understand how the simplest misunderstanding had somehow awakened within her more insecurities than she knew she had.

It wasn't about the misunderstanding to her. To Amber, this was about abandonment, injustice, lack of honor, irony, and deceit. To Amber, this was about past lifetimes of pain in which she had been killed based on assumptions or accusations others made on her behalf. Countless past lives in which, if somebody wished to see her go down, they would accuse her until her death was granted by to those who wished her evil. It sounds dramatic, but many people who feel resonance to spiritual concepts, healing, and energy work have been through similar scenarios. The clear majority of healers in the world have been exposed to scenarios like witch huntings from the past and being burned or hanged due to their spiritual abilities, which were persecuted back in the day. Those fears remain within the subconscious mind and need to be addressed for healing to take place.

Oftentimes, people don't remember these memories in their conscious minds, but they can feel intense emotional triggers if exposed to something in this lifetime that reminds them, at a soul level, of the pain they have been through before.

To Amber, what was being triggered had nothing to do with Simone and everything to do with her past. She was not the one known to succumb to other people's opinions. She was not the one to give power to others that way, but here, she had fallen so in love with the group, with the experience, and with the feeling of having a teacher to look up to that it broke her. To be ripped off from that with no clear explanation was excruciating for her.

She felt like her whole sense of confidence and security had been ripped from her hands. The illusion and innocence that had begun to blossom again within her seemed crushed.

Amber's real healing process had begun. Every fear she held of not being good enough to continue her path was triggered for her to put into practice all she had learned. It seemed like the Universe had designed the master event to push all of Amber's buttons simultaneously.

She felt confused and cloudy daily. She thought she was just angry at Simone. She thought she was just really hurt. She needed healing for a process bigger and wider than she had ever contemplated. What happened with Simone was the catalyst she needed for change. How could she call herself a healer, after all, if she couldn't heal herself?

CHAPTER 33

Amber developed a lot of fears after Simone pointed out so many of her supposed flaws so loudly and intensely. A part of her trusted Simone so much that she began to wonder if it was all true. A seed was planted in her mind—the seed of doubt. She wondered several times if it could be possible that she was not seeing something about herself that was obvious to the rest of the group. She questioned her ego. She questioned her intentions. She even questioned her plans of continuing the path of healing for the world around her. As her career sped up, she asked herself if it was possible she just enjoyed the spotlight. She questioned many of her thoughts and actions only to realize these fears were getting in the way.

She had not understood at which point she had given so much power to Simone's opinion. She never thought such a simple disagreement could continue to linger on her mind, even months after it had happened.

She was surprised to find herself doubting her abilities, questioning herself endlessly, and beginning to play small again. If Simone was jealous, like Victoria had implied countless times, she had gotten exactly what she wanted. Amber had become inevitably doubtful in her physical reality. Since she had begun to resent Simone, the feelings somehow evolved, she began resenting certain aspects about shamanism.

She felt offended after realizing there were so many people out there who weren't walking the talk. She continued to feel betrayed, thinking her teacher, the one who implied Amber wasn't impeccable enough, didn't even seem to know the meaning of that word. She was just so disappointed about it all, especially after observing how the group began to drift away from her, rejecting her without having the slightest clue of what had happened or giving her a chance to explain. No one even asked. They just drifted, trusting whatever Simone chose to tell them.

There was an aspect of comedy to the whole issue. It was so ridiculous in the most basic, human, and rudimentary manner, independent of the spiritually rich environment in which it happened. That goes to prove that no matter how spiritually evolved people consider themselves to be, self-mastery is a lifelong journey. It also goes to prove that, people don't need to go through big massive tragedies to have their hearts shattered.

Oftentimes, people think that, only if they go through massive loss or heartbreak are they qualified to seek help. Small things can have a powerful effect on the way people see themselves and the world around them. As people develop a higher awareness over themselves, they realize the huge impact certain events can have over the mind. It's important to learn to love oneself enough to cater even the smallest wounds.

People are divine beings, and they are supposed to feel in complete harmony and abundance most of the time. Because people are divine beings living a physical experience, it is natural to experience emotional ups and downs. However, if a person does not feel in harmony within the mind, most of the time, that person has the right and the responsibility to observe what is going on.

Months continued to pass, and Amber's fears and insecurities would come and go. She continued to clear the negative energies from that wound in all the ways she knew how. Something was still held within her, regardless of her attempts to heal. As she went through her days and her patients' therapies, she wouldn't think about it at all anymore, just like any other old relationship. Life began happening without it, and it was slowly left behind.

Healing comes in different shapes and forms. Healing can be as easy as an instant shift that can happen in a second, and healing comes, just like that. Sometimes the healing process only serves one purpose, which is to teach something. As soon as an individual realizes what it is he or she needs to learn, the person heals instantly.

Sometimes, people try and try, finding it's not that easy. Sometimes the lesson is not that apparent, even for those consciously looking for it. Time needs to go by and new perspectives need to be introduced into life for people to truly grasp what it is that is trying to get across to them.

Amber continued trying to be impartial, and she tried to give credit to Simone as much as she could. Over time, she realized out of love for herself that she needed to be a bit more observant. Not everyone was who they claimed to be, and not everyone deserved her respect.

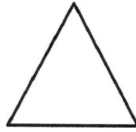

CHAPTER 34

It was ten o'clock on a Tuesday morning in Panama City. Victoria decided to visit Amber after her countless requests asking her to do so. Once she got there, she found Amber to be quite irritated and confused.

"What's wrong?" Victoria asked, concerned when she realized how stressed Amber looked sitting on the corner of her bed.

"I'm not sure, but I think I will be needing your help." Amber glanced up at her, looking embarrassed to even ask in the first place.

"Yeah, sure. What's wrong?" Victoria asked again as she sat down next to Amber.

"Okay, so I am regularly having about five patients a week pretty consistently. Last week, everyone began to cancel on me. I had five therapies scheduled and confirmed last week, and they all fell through. It is so odd, because this never happens. Yesterday's patient also cancelled at the last minute. It's very frustrating. I don't know what is happening," Amber confided.

"Do you think this is somehow a reflection of you?" Victoria looked at her, trying to guess her point of view.

"Well, yeah, I guess. I have been feeling very inadequate lately. I have somehow began doubting myself to the point of exhaustion." Amber looked embarrassed after admitting feeling that way. "According to the law of attraction, what you are feeling is reflected in your general energy frequency, and then the way your energy is vibrating becomes what you attract. I have been feeling useless, and somehow the Universe seems to be reflecting that to me by making all patients agree?" She immediately looked sad with her realization.

"Do you really think that's it?" Victoria laughed compassionately at her troubled friend.

"I don't know, but I would love to figure it out. I thought maybe you could give me a healing therapy." Amber's looked shifted to a small smile as she tried to convince Victoria to perform a healing therapy on her right then and there.

"I thought you were inviting me to meditate or do something fun when you said I should bring all of my shamanic stuff." Victoria continued to laugh, giving in to her friend's request. "Okay. Let me open sacred space. I'll help you out."

Victoria began to arrange all the sacred objects she was carrying in her special white bag decorated with golden images of elephants and flowers. She placed all her tools next to her and got herself ready.

Amber lay down, relieved to know that if there

was anything indeed wrong, Victoria would help her. Shamanic healing therapies can inform and purify the system even if a person isn't completely clear on what is it she wishes to work on. Usually, whatever is keeping the person blocked will come to the surface as the healing experience begins.

"To the winds of the south, Great Serpent," Victoria began praying out loud as she faced south. "Wrap your coils of light around us. Teach us how to shed the past the way you shed your skin, to walk softly on the earth. Teach us to walk in the path of beauty and purity.

"To the winds of the west, Mother Jaguar, protect our medicine space. Teach us the way of the peaceful warrior, the one which holds no enemies. Teach us to live impeccably.

"To the winds of the north, Hummingbird, Grandmother, and Grandfather, Ancestors, come and warm your hands by our fires. Whisper to us in the wind. We honor who have come before us and who will come after us, our children's children.

"To the winds of the east, Great Eagle, Condor. Come to us from the place of the rising sun. Keep us under your wings. Show us the mountains we have only dare to dream of. Teach us to fly side by side with the Great Spirit.

"Mother Earth, we've gathered here for the healing of all of your children, the stone people, the plant people, the four-legged, the two-legged, the crawlers, the finned, the furred, and the winged ones. All of our relationships—we are all one.

"Father Sun, Grandmother Moon, to the star nations,

Great Spirit, you are known by a thousand names, and you who are really the unnamable one. Thank you for bringing us together to sing the song of life."

Every time Amber listened to that prayer, her heart would feel blessed and her soul would expand in hope and beauty. A part of her, deeper than she could understand, remembered those words. An ancient part of her had said that prayer countless times before on behalf of lifetimes filled with patients and tribe members seeking help. Amber felt relaxed as a sense of complete surrender covered her body, which was lying down on a black yoga mat on the floor in her bedroom. Victoria began to harmonize the space using sage incense, drums, and additional prayers. Once she was ready, Victoria sat down crossed-legged on the floor next to her friend, ready to begin.

"How can I help you today, beautiful patient?" Victoria asked, showing a profound sense of peace.

"Well, like I mentioned, I need to know if there's anything within me that is blocking patients from coming to their scheduled appointments. I continue to feel impeccable with my intentions, but I'm feeling insecure and doubtful. I don't want to feel like that anymore. It's exhausting and unfair," Amber said, beginning to feel annoyed again by the whole situation.

"Why does it seem unfair to you?" Victoria asked as she opened her mesa, her portable altar made of a rich folded fabric, which held her khuyas, or healing stones.

"It's unfair, because I never intended to hurt anyone. All I have ever had in mind was the well-being of everyone, and I don't understand how I was dragged into this situation. Everything was going so perfectly, and now the whole group has begun to drift away from me … judging me, when for a full year, not judging was one of the most important principles. I feel rejected. I feel judged." Amber's eyes began to water again, and she allowed it with no resistance, as she understood that crying is the purification of the soul. "People who I honestly felt were friends are just drifting away from me with no apparent reason and without me understanding anything. I somehow let down Simone, and she never gave me a chance to explain anything to her or to anyone else. Everyone is assuming things on my behalf when all I have ever wanted was to be impeccable and to serve …" Amber cried hopelessly, allowing her pain to be shown completely. She realized there was more left to heal than she had known. As she wiped her tears from her eyes, she looked at Victoria for comfort.

"I know … It really has been unfortunate how it all happened, but I'm pretty sure you can turn it into a learning experience or growth. I know it seems like it won't get better, but it will, and you have control over all your decisions. You are responsible for what you do, not how others interpret what you do. You know in your heart your intentions have always been pure." Victoria held her patient's arm compassionately, letting her know she understood her pain.

"How has this whole thing made you feel?" Victoria asked.

"I feel exposed … judged … humiliated … confused … enraged … hopeless … offended," Amber said, leaving a few seconds to think between each emotion expressed.

"Which one of those would you say is the strongest emotion you have felt? The one that hurts the most." Victoria flowed gracefully through the usual questions a shamanic practitioner would ask a patient.

"I feel enraged to have to live consequences based on assumptions others make about me, leaving me without any possibility to express who I really am or my true intentions," Amber said, feeling a knot in her heart chakra beginning to form.

"Enraged," Victoria said, staring at a distance as she accidentally began feeling Amber's rage within her own body.

Flashbacks of different scenes from what seemed like Amber's past lifetimes began popping into Victoria's mind. In a flash second she understood that the reason this was so impossibly hard for Amber was because in her past lives as a healer, she had been persecuted and killed unfairly, many times. Knowing this, Victoria proceeded carefully, as she continued to ask the standard questions required to go deeper into the patient's emotions.

"Behind the feeling of rage and anger, what can you find?" Victoria continued to stare at a distance while Amber's tears kept coming.

"I mean … honestly, I feel really abandoned and alone," Amber admitted, allowing her heart to crack open. Her realization made her feel an intense sense of hopelessness. She began to grieve the whole situation and how the most magical experience of her entire life ended up becoming another wound to address alongside all the other painful moments in her life.

Victoria asked Amber for a hug without the need for

words, and as she embraced her, Amber remembered how everything that happened to her was divinely designed for her to grow, evolve, and heal. Amber began honoring her pain as a teacher instead of a punishment.

"It's funny how we can know all the theoretical aspects of something, yet when we most need that understanding, it feels impossible to find." Amber began giggling as she wiped away her last tears.

"What do you mean?" Victoria laughed as she realized how messed up Amber looked. Her eyes were puffy and red.

"I mean, I know that right now I'm completely caught up in a victim mentality, but I really feel like it's unfair, you know? I'm controlled by it. I also know that this was all orchestrated to teach me something. I know nothing's an error; every single thing that happens, happens in divine order and alignment to help us evolve and grow. My brain knows this, but my heart doesn't seem to agree with any of it. It feels so real and so excruciatingly painful," Amber explained, adding a funny tone to the whole conversation.

"Well, we have graduated, but becoming a shaman is a lifelong journey. How can you say you can heal others if you can't, yet, heal yourself?" Victoria answered back, exposing the same insight Amber had received before, countless times.

CHAPTER 35

The healing therapy continued, and Victoria proceeded to clear, balance, and harmonize Amber's chakra system. After that, she went into a procedure called extraction of crystallized energies, which allows solidified energy from past life wounds and painful events to be removed. Victoria had become an incredible, compassionate, and loving healer. She had been there for Amber, allowing her to really open up and get it all out in order to heal.

Victoria placed her intention out loud for the ideal crystallized energies within Amber's body to get activated, letting them both know where they were and how to remove them. Right before Victoria finished her intention setting, Amber's hands began to feel itchy. Her palms were experiencing all sorts of tickles, sensations, and energy movement. She started laughing, enjoying the immediate effect of the intention placed. She told Victoria what she was feeling, and as Amber opened her eyes with a smile on her face, she found Victoria with an expression of disgust in hers.

"What is it?" Amber laughed nervously. "What do you see?"

"Ew!" Victoria said out loud. "Your hands are infested with what looks like tiny worms—thousands and thousands of them. God, this is disgusting!"

"Ew, really?" Amber's smiled faded instantly as she looked at her hands, only feeling the tickles and movements of what did feel like tiny worms biting her skin.

They both looked at each other with faces of horror and without the need of words decided to continue the therapy. Victoria went through the whole procedure about two to three times, realizing they were almost impossible to remove. Every time Victoria felt like she was done, Amber began to feel the tickles on a different finger or specific area, as if one of the tiny worms was left behind. Victoria began to get annoyed and decided to get rid of them at all costs. She pulled out of her bag sticks of sage, selenite crystal wands, essential oils, and her rattle. She spent a good half hour cleaning Amber's hands thoroughly, until she could finally move on to the next procedure. They were both exhausted, but figured they might as well go through one longer, well-done clearing rather than having to repeat the encounter again. The whole time Amber felt relaxed, but she continued to hear the laughter of a woman in the back of her mind. She wondered for a while what could it possibly be but ceased to try after not receiving any intuitive guidance about it.

"It's probably because of how many patients I have

been treating. Maybe my hands just got, you know, dirty. Maybe I need to have a special treatment for them or protect them in a different way," Amber surmised aloud.

"Yeah, we can figure out some steps for you to protect them in the future. They are your biggest asset. Through them, the light comes out of you as a channel and into patients. If your hands are in this condition, the Universe won't allow any patients to come to you, and rightfully so. We need to be very grateful that the message was received clearly, and I'm happy you asked for my help." Victoria smiled, grabbing Amber's arm lovingly. "It's also great that it's clear now why your patients have been cancelling, and now your therapy schedule will come back to normal."

"Yeah, I can't wait." Amber smiled. "I can't explain to you how much I enjoy the time with my patients. It gives me a sense of purpose I haven't found anywhere else."

"Yeah, I know what you mean." Victoria smiled as she began putting all her tools back into her bag, indicating Amber they would continue right away.

In a modern society, people tend to cover their wounds as soon as they happen. They are covered, suppressed, and kept out of sight. People do this rapidly because they need to be functional, and they can't allow pain to get in the way of daily living. The wounds are hidden so fast, but people don't take the time to observe if they are infected before putting them away. Just like a physical wound: if the skin grows over an infected area, even though it's covered, what's underneath the skin can bring great harm to the body. It is not healed. During healing therapies, people intend to open the wound again and clean everything by reliving it, addressing it, and exchanging the pain for love. Only after a profound cleansing of the previously infected area can a person really call herself healed.

After that procedure, Victoria explained to Amber how she would go even deeper and guide her through a fluid energy extraction procedure to see if there were any entities, earthbound spirits, or dense energies within her system. This is the one in which any form of foreign dense energy within the patient's body would be guided into a special crystal, thereby liberating Amber, in this case, from the negative effects of what could be entities, earthbound spirits, negative influences, curses, etc. Amber had begun to feel a little bit lightheaded and tired after what had already been one hour of therapy.

"Okay, doll. Let's check if you have any foreign stuff within you, shall we?" Victoria began to stand up and indicated that Amber should do the same.

"I feel super lightheaded, Vic." Amber laughed as she stood up. Her light-blue bedroom seemed prettier than usual.

"Have you been drinking water? Remember that before any form of healing therapy, you need to be really hydrated," Victoria answered automatically as she would for any other patient.

"Vic, I do this for a living, remember?" Amber laughed again, reminding her she knew the whole therapy by heart.

Victoria laughed at her automatic response and realized a lot of her patients felt lightheaded to the point that she would immediately answer back to their comments without even processing it. Victoria grabbed her mesa and the special crystal wand that was held within a bright-red pouch with a black interior.

"I feel really lightheaded, Vic, seriously," Amber insisted, sitting on the corner of the bed.

"What do you feel?"

"I'm hearing someone laughing … It sounds like the voice of a woman laughing." Amber's head began pounding. She embraced her head in her hands and allowed the moment to pass by, feeling better almost immediately.

"What was that?" Amber asked as she looked up to Victoria, who was still standing up and concerned about her as she kept the extraction crystal in hand.

"I have no idea …" Victoria waited for guidance from her spirit guides without receiving any instant intuitive messages. "Let's continue and see what pops up for you further into the therapy …"

Amber nodded, and they began the whole extraction process. After using a specific muscle-testing technique, Victoria confirmed the existence of some form of foreign energy within Amber's system. Once the confirmation was received, they could move on to the next step: the actual extraction. They were both standing up, facing each other. Amber's hands rested over Victoria's, and their arms were relaxed. They said a prayer, placed their clear intentions for the process, and closed their eyes. Amber breathed deeply, allowing her mind to relax to be fully open to receive the benefits of the therapy. Victoria visualized the energy and began interacting with it at a telepathic level to move it out of Amber's system and into the healing crystal. The crystal was held tightly between their left hands. Their fingers kept the crystal secured in place.

Shivers began to run all over Amber's skin, and she felt her skin becoming quite cold. She began to feel like she was, suddenly, experiencing a high fever. Her mind got cloudy as she began to hear the feminine voice laughing in her mind again. The voice became louder and louder, and her physical sensations became increasingly unpleasant. Amber opened her eyes for a second to find Victoria with her eyes closed, completely focused on what she was doing. Her face looked tense, and Amber could clearly see it was not the right time to interrupt her.

Amber closed her eyes again, and as soon as she did, in her mind, she saw Simone. She saw her, blowing what seemed like dry leaves, which were grey and black, out of her own hand and over to Amber as she laughed. As soon as she saw Simone blowing these energies onto her, she began to feel worse. Simone's laughter began to grow louder and louder, making it impossible for her to close her eyes anymore. It was really disturbing for her. She opened and closed her eyes several times, impatient regarding when Victoria was going to extract whatever Simone had apparently sent her way.

A few seconds went by, and Amber relaxed again, closing her eyes and trying to remain calm after the confusing realizations. As she closed her eyes again, the image of Simone began to disappear, as if it were fading away slowly. As soon as she disappeared completely from Amber's mind, so did all the physical symptoms she was experiencing. At that exact same second, Victoria pulled the crystal that was being held between their hands. Victoria pulled the crystal violently and immediately looked for the red velvet bag to put it in it. She looked exhausted.

"What was that?" Victoria widened her eyes, alarmed by the strength of the energy she had just guided into the crystal.

"It was Simone." Amber sat down on the corner of the bed again, looking as confused as she looked disappointed.

"What?" Victoria sat down next to her as she covered herself in rose water, trying to dissipate the feeling of the dense energy on her skin.

"As you were guiding the energy out of me, I began to feel incredibly sick. I began to feel as if I had a fever. It was strong. I didn't say anything, because you looked really focused. I began hearing the loud voice of a woman laughing again. This time when I closed my eyes, I clearly saw Simone blowing what seemed like a curse on to me. She laughed as she blew dark black and grey energies all over me. She seemed to be really enjoying it too." Amber looked at Victoria in awe of what she had seen.

"Damn. That's intense, Amber." Victoria grabbed her hand, shocked to hear what Amber had to say. "Are you sure?"

"Believe me, I'm sure. It was undeniable. Goodness gracious, what a mess." Amber's exhausted body fell over the mattress, as Victoria continued to sit next to her.

They spent some minutes in silence, not knowing exactly what everything meant or how to fix it. They both wondered if Simone was conscious of this and if she intended to mess with Amber in such a direct and shameless way. They continued to wonder if the sweet woman they had spent time with for a full year, learning about the light of love and how to use it could be capable of such manipulative behavior. They both wondered if it was something she planned to continue doing. If so, Amber would need to find a way to protect herself from it.

CHAPTER 36

She held that phrase in her mind for a few days until Amber decided to ask for assistance from the spirit world. She would contact her guides one more time to seek advice. She decided to take some time for meditation and got herself ready, closed her eyes, and allowed the experience to unfold.

Amber's mind began to hold the image of a magical pine tree forest as she meditated crossed-legged, sitting on her bedroom's Moroccan-looking meditation pillow. The floor in her vision was covered with a white, thick, and peaceful-looking snow. The sky was grey, and snow continued to fall over the enchanted scene as she noticed that, from a distance, a pack of wolves began to approach her, leaving their paw prints on the thick snow carpet behind them. They walked over to her shyly, respectfully but without fear.

She stood there as the wolves in her vision came closer, and while she looked at them, her heart began to fill with a deep sense of belonging. She felt at home with them. She felt like she had shared with them for eons before that moment. There was one who had different colored eyes; one was green and one was blue. With that wolf, she felt an intense magnetic pull, and she couldn't help embracing him as he came closer. Tears began to flow as she experienced a profound love she had never experienced in her physical reality.

As she kneeled with one knee in the snow, embracing this wolf, her familiar spirit guide, Master Wolf, began to appear from thin air, behind the pack. His size was considerably bigger, allowing it to be clear to her that he was the leader of the pack. He continued to walk slowly and magnificently toward her, opening space between the other wolves.

She stood up again to face him. He sat down in front of her, and she looked up to him. He was way larger than any wolf found in ordinary reality, and he was mighty and strong. His grey fur danced as the frozen air caressed them both. His eyes were tender, loving, and kind.

Amber began to feel his energy expanding, vibrating in such a tangible way that she became lightheaded in her physical body, which still sat crossed-legged in her bedroom. In her vision, she fell to her knees, overwhelmed with the great power he exuded. She bowed to him and honored his existence and his grace.

"I have a lot to share with you today, Amber." His authoritative voice appeared in her mind.

"I really appreciate anything you can share with me.

I need guidance. Please, share with me the next right action," Amber pleaded kindly, feeling cared for.

"You always hold the choice of how you'd like to act. You hold the power to choose every single time with every single situation, if you'd like to act or react. It only takes a second to pause and allow our higher awareness to come in. There will be times when you will find yourself in situations that seem to touch a nerve within you so painfully that acting seems impossible, yet reacting feels like a relief. When you can acknowledge, you acted the best you knew how always, you will feel peace looking back." The wolf began standing on his four paws again. He began walking slowly and encouraged Amber to walk beside him, over the snow.

"It is easy to admire other people for their wisdom, their expertise, or their knowledge. Admiring and appreciating people's gifts to the world is a beautiful way to receive inspiration; however, it's very easy for you all to create a sense of separation from those you admire. When you think, even for a second, that another person is more special than you, in any way, you create distance between that person and yourself. By placing them on pedestals, consciously or unconsciously, we create distance between who we are and who we'd like to become. All the people around us whom we admire reflect our own light." The wolf continued to share with her, patiently.

Amber continued to walk beside him with her hands inside her faded jeans pockets. In the vision, she wore a thick knitted beige scarf that covered her chest and neck. Her soft brown hair was pushed beneath a matching knitted hat. Her nose was red, and as she breathed, smoke would escape her gracefully shaped lips due to the cold.

"Behind every act of violence one can partake in, voluntarily or involuntarily, there's pain. What is happening with Simone defines her. How you react to it defines you. This exposes a side of her that needs healing. She can choose to see it that way and evolve, or she can choose to remain in her ego and be forced to receive a similar situation to work with in the future. Unhealed past repeats itself until it's healed. The same goes for you. You, just like her, have a lot of perspectives to heal to leave these issues behind.

Know that when people engage in violent behaviors toward you, that is not a reflection of you, it's the reflection of them. How much you are triggered reflects you. The thing is, you hold the power of alchemy. You can transform the energy that is sent your way into a sacred energy. A wound has the potential to become the equivalent of a trophy after you choose to consciously act based on your highest truth and deal with it from love instead of fear. It becomes a sacred lesson that, when shared, serves humanity. Your choices, rather than your circumstances, are the ones that will define you."

They both stared at the dark entrance of what seemed like a rocky cave ahead on their path. They stood outside of the small and mysterious crack in the mountain, right underneath a massive pine tree that was tall enough for them to stand underneath it comfortably.

"Let's sit here for a second. I will explain to you a

bit more about what we will be doing." The wolf made himself comfortable and sat next to the trunk of the tree.

Amber hadn't spoken a word. She was trying to soak up as much wisdom as she could from the spirit guide's words. She followed him and sat next to him, close enough for him to keep her warm. Her physical body was beginning to feel uncomfortable back in her bedroom. She moved around her legs to change sitting positions but never opened her eyes, fearing the vividness of the vision would be affected.

"When you feel this way—hurt, betrayed, and broken—find within yourself the power of love," he continued.

"Could you please share with me how to do this? I have never intended to feel such a load of harmful emotions. I have really tried to keep my center lately, but I have found it to be so hard. I have felt rage, anger, and such profound disappointment," she asked, openly admitting her process to the wolf.

"You find a way to feel compassion for the person you are dealing with. Simone, for example—she has had years of spiritual studies, knowledge, experience, and guidance. She knows what she must do and how to do it; however, she is experiencing so much pain right now that it has opened the door for ego, fear, and lack to enter her mind. She, like you, is doing the best she can." Wolf looked into Amber's eyes, tilting his head to the side and coming closer to her, allowing her to integrate that compassion into her being. Spirit guides can heal, they can lend their energies for those of others to rise, allowing those they are helping to enter a state in which the right perspective is easier to attain. Suddenly, Amber was filled with a profound sense of love toward Simone. Everything within her was shifting; she could feel it. It was the kind of love that holds no judgment, the kind of love that is grateful for everything that happens, the kind of love that heals.

"Will you take the energy she has sent to you and transform it into love, which you will send her way?" Wolf asked as what seemed like a smile was drawn across his face.

"There's nothing I'd like to do more. I have tried, but it doesn't seem to work, at least not from the way I've been attempting." Amber smiled honestly as she leaned on to his massive build, glaring at the sky, which began to shift colors for the next few seconds. Just like northern lights, they shifted from pink to purple and from purple to yellow into a mix of all colors adorning the sky. They leaned against each other in silence, enjoying the magic of a new realization—one that had never been conscious before for Amber. She had been so busy feeling like Simone was being unreasonable, unfair, insane, and rude that she hadn't had any time to think about the pain the could be behind her behavior.

"You see that cave?" the wolf asked, breaking the silence. "You will go in there, understand what the next years will bring and come back healed. If you don't heal, you don't come out."

"What do you mean, I don't come out? What about my physical body?" Amber asked, confused.

"Your body will fall asleep if it needs to, and no matter how long it takes, you don't come out until you are completely healed. Do you understand?" Wolf stood up again, and the pack of wolves began to approach them both from a distance. They had walked together a great distance, leaving the pack behind. Master Wolf began to slowly disappear, looking more transparent with every second that went by.

"How can I know if I'm completely healed?" Amber asked him with an urgent tone of voice as she realized he was disappearing.

"Master!" she insisted loudly, realizing he was completely gone.

She stood there in silence, looking at how the pack walked peacefully her way. There were seven wolves, all grey except for one, which was white. She admired them from a distance and wondered if maybe they could guide her into a deeper understanding of what she was supposed to do. As they arrived closer to her, she could feel a magnetic pull to that one wolf. He had different colored eyes and his fur was white, making him physically different than all the others. He stood at the back of the pack, and they all stared at her, peacefully.

"You can only be called a shaman if you learn to heal yourself every time," said one of the wolves as they all began walking closer and closer to her, pushing her gently into entering the cave. The sky turned dark, covered with dark clouds, and violent winds forecasting the importance this moment would present for her path. Amber looked around at the somber scene and began feeling fear rise within her.

"What do I need to do in there? Could anybody explain to me?" Amber asked with a sense of urgency as she continued to be pushed closer to the cave by the wolves. They were forcing her to walk backward, away from them.

The wolves' eyes became pitch-black and made her feel fear of them for the first time. Her instinctual response was to become alert of her surroundings and see if there was anything she could defend herself with in case they attacked her. She stood no chance against a pack of angry wolves. If they wanted to hurt her, they would.

Her back landed abruptly on the mountain's rock wall, right next to the crack entrance to the cave. She began breathing deeply, trying to regain her center before going in. She closed her eyes as the wolves surrounded her, beginning to growl at her and showing their teeth aggressively. She could feel their penetrating gaze on her, even with her eyes closed. She felt the same amount of fear she used to experience with the horrible hauntings and nightmares. She experienced an enormous amount of resistance to go into the cave. She was certain that the last time she would see Simone would be in that cave.

CHAPTER 37

Drops of water fell to the ground, and their sound echoed across the darkness of the cave. There was complete silence filling the moments in between each drop falling to the dusty floor. Amber couldn't see her hand in front of her if she tried. She walked carefully in the darkness, stretching her arms around her to avoid crashing face-first into a wall.

As she continued to walk around the sometimes narrow, sometimes wide spaces within the huge cave, she realized the shape of the raw stone looked, within the darkness, like it had figures naturally carved within it. Out of the corner of her eye, she would see the image of a man, but when she turned to look, there was no one there. She would see his silhouette drawn on the texture of the rock walls appearing from time to time. It made her nervous.

"You have arrived." She heard the wolf's voice in her mind.

As she approached the light entering a side of the cave, it became brighter and brighter. It was a sky-blue glow that exuded kindness and loving energy. She began to feel relieved as she walked closer and stood on the edge of the stone floor, observing the beautiful scene in front of her. The rock pathway began to expand into a huge open space. As Amber stood in amazement of the beauty of this space, tiny blue lights seemed to twinkle around what seemed like an enchanted forest. Fireflies began appearing everywhere—around the tall trees, around the wild bushes filled with flowers, and around the foggy atmosphere in general. The sound of harps began to sound at a distance, and she felt like she had stumbled upon heaven itself.

She entered the space respectfully, understanding the magic taking place in that scene. She asked permission as she entered, as she usually did, by taking a strand of her own hair and offering it as a peaceful gift to the energies of the space. She walked around in amusement of the inexplicable beauty around her. Fairies began to appear gently around her, looking like little orbs of pink, purple, and sky-blue light. They played around her, moved her silky brown hair, and giggled as she smiled with their appearance.

"You are here to heal, Amber," a loving female voice expressed.

"I'm ready," Amber answered back, feeling all her fear dissolve in the presence of all the flowers and butterflies adorning the space.

"Do you know why you were brought here exactly?" the voice asked.

"I know I need to forgive myself and Simone for everything that has happened. I know I need to leave the pain behind forever to continue my path."

"You will meet with her here, and then you will continue on to an even deeper healing experience." the voice replied.

The powerful statement made Amber's skin feel magnetic, and naturally, she began to seek the origin of this voice.

"Your "higher self" resides within you. It is the highest and purest version of you—the almighty godlike energy within you. Your higher self knows the path to follow, knows the mission and mistakes nothing, while it recognizes only love," the voice continued.

"You are here to allow that light and wisdom within you to take over your human experience and body permanently, bringing you into your becoming. You are here to forgive Simone, yes. But on a wider scale, you are here to forgive all there is, including yourself and everything you have ever experienced as a soul on this planet." The voice continued coming from all over the space.

Amber found herself, suddenly, dressed in a long white flowing dress and bare feet. The ground was moist beneath her feet, and the foggy weather was fresh with the scent of nature. She touched her head and found that she was wearing a crown made with wild flowers and leaves. Simultaneously, she began walking slowly and looking around the space in search of the voice she was hearing.

"You will now meet with your teacher. Do you see that crystal pyramid over there?" the voice said calmly.

"Yes," Amber answered, feeling a bit intimidated by the encounter.

"You will walk in there and sit with Simone until you truly understand what is happening," the figure continued.

Amber immediately pulled her dress up a bit to allow her feet to walk freely over the mud as she headed toward the crystal pyramid. It was high enough for a tall person to stand within it, but there wasn't much space for anything else. The walls were made of completely transparent crystal quartz. As she walked closer, she could see through the crystal that Simone was sitting cross-legged inside and was wearing a white dress as well. Amber paused just before entering the narrow opening in the crystal wall and took a deep breath. She had been controlled by so many feelings of confusion, rage, disappointment, and sadness due to the way everything had turned out between them.

She stepped into the pyramid carefully and was immediately impressed by the complete silence and harmonious energy inside. She felt instantly serene and detached from all those heavy emotions. The temperature inside the pyramid was cold and pleasant. The space was infused with the scent of roses, and the lighting was golden and gentle. Amber took a few seconds to enjoy the atmosphere and then faced Simone, who was sitting with her eyes closed, as though she hadn't heard Amber coming in. They sat across from each other in complete surrender to the energy of love surrounding them. There was no tension, no thoughts—there was just love.

After a few minutes, Simone opened her eyes to meet Amber's. Both smiled gently and nodded at each other humbly.

"I am here to explain to you why I'm doing what I'm doing," Simone said slowly.

Amber remained silent, remembering the difficult times she had been going through, which were all, in one way or another, related to her.

"You see, in our physical reality, I have been nothing but disrespectful to you. I have offended you to your face and discredited you behind your back. I have constantly drained you, manipulate you, and placed spells on you. I have. It's true. This will continue for years. My shadows will do everything in their power to bring you down and when I mean everything, I mean everything. But I need you to understand the truth," Simone explained confidently.

"What is that truth?" Amber asked, looking confused and disappointed again.

"The truth is that teachers take on a big responsibility. Their mission is to teach and prepare their students to the best of their ability. Sometimes that happens in our human reality, and sometimes it happens *through* our human reality," Simone continued.

"What's the difference between the two?" Amber questioned her.

"If I were to teach you in our human reality, I would give you classes and lectures, literally teaching you the material I want you to learn. If I were to teach you through human experience, you will be learning lessons through the experiences I put you through. The truth is, Amber, that I assumed the responsibility of being one of your teachers in this life. Good teachers don't mind if their students end up resenting them or hating them. They trust that if the teaching comes across, they are doing what's right for the higher good of that student. Our souls agreed upon this before coming here. Nothing is a mistake. I'm sacrificing my image so I can continue to teach you. The image you have of me is tainted and stained by all sorts of illusions. I know how much disappointment you have felt, and I'm okay with it. This whole experience has taught you more about yourself than the course ever did. I'm on your side, cheering for you, even if it doesn't seem that way. It may seem like chaos in the reality we are both living in, but remember, all those crazy things I've done to you are nothing but opportunities for you to evolve. I'm paying so much attention to you, lovingly. Can't you see that? If I didn't care for you, I would have just disappeared from your life. I would have given up. But I care so much that I've allowed emotions like jealousy, greed, and despair move me and created all sorts of scenarios for you to become the best you can be. I know how to handle myself. I have chosen not to, for you," Simone said patiently.

As Amber sat quietly listening to Simone's words, tears began to fill her eyes, and this time, they were tears of joy.

"Through the years to come, the attacks will get worse. There will come a time in which my power won't be enough so I will hire others to take your power and energy away, basically to stop you through black magic. My ego will write checks my soul can't cash and there will be deep consequences for me. Through the years, I will speak poorly of you and like a sneaky spy, I will find my way through your life until you learn how to raise your vibration and protect yourself like a pro. Your mission is big, Amber. I will put you through hell now, so when your mission begins, you are ready. You will see the rise of me and the fall. You will see me succeeding, taking your powers and energy if you allow me to. You won't be the only one I betray. You will see my rise and you will have to endure seeing my fall which will be painful to watch. You will run into angels which will assist you, in human form. It won't be easy, Amber, but you need to understand the truth and keep it close to your heart. Through this, you will understand your power and most importantly, your mission." Simone explained coldly.

"How can you know this and manage to do these things?" Amber looked impressed as she cleared the tears from her eyes.

"Oh, I will not know. I will intellectualize and rationalize my motifs. I will be, according to me, protecting shamanism but truly just trying to get rid of what my human selves perceives to be competition. No one can bring down Simone, I will tell myself. The thing is someone can and that is, myself. I will manage to do just that, impressively. I will be a puppet to my shadows, feeling empowered in my ignorance. I will honestly believe I am teaching you a valuable lesson by punishing you. I will be drunk on the power the darkness has bestowed on me. It goes even deeper Amber. The darkness will be working thorough me, as me, so will be the light. My soul is training you, my ego trying to stop you. See the paradox? My soul is preparing you for what the darkness is trying to stop, your mission. This universe, among multiverses, is way more complex than our human mind can see at first sight. That's why we are here." Simone explained.

"Wow... I don't know what to say" Amber looked helpless.

"After going through this, you will fully understand how pure you truly are. I will tempt you. I will give you so many opportunities and invitations to take the bait and engage in a competition for power. You will have the perfect chance to destroy me and you will choose not to. This has all been planned before. You are bigger than that. You are wiser than that. You are above this human nonsense and you know it. Yes, it will be excruciating both physically and emotionally but you will come out on the other side and well, I will not. Be grateful for the position you have on this lesson. You may feel like a victim but the true disgrace will come to me and not you. I choose to do this out of love." Simone admitted proudly.

"Why does it has to happen this way?" Amber knew this to be true, she could feel it coming.

"You are being started young because there's a lot to do. This tough years will be kept in your youth but your mastery will prevail for the rest of your life. I love you will all my heart and I just want you to know, it must be this way. Don't try to talk me out of it, don't try to stop me in human reality. Don't even try to help me when it all comes crashing down for me. Let it be. If it's prison, allow it. If it's sickness, allow it. I will use everything I know to avoid consequences but the bill will come, it always does, just allow it. Now, because of all of this, you will receive a gift right now. Your heart chakra will be replaced and you will get a new one, you know, so you can endure more pain" Simone whispered compassionately as she began to fade away.

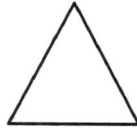

CHAPTER 38

"What happened?" Amber whispered, opening her heavy eyelids.

She looked confused as she lay on her own bed with her white pajamas on and wrapped in thick blankets. Her bedroom was cold, yet the smell of a vanilla-scented candle made it feel nice enough.

As she looked around, she saw Sarah, her sister, sitting on a chair next to her bed. Sarah looked tired. In her bedroom, she also saw Victoria leaning against the wall, as if they were checking up on her. Amber's mom sat next to Sarah. It seemed like they had been waiting for her to wake up for a while. As she woke up, they all came closer to Amber. Sarah sat on the edge of her bed and smiled gently at Amber.

"You passed out while you were meditating," Sarah told her. "We drove you to the emergency room, but they didn't find anything wrong with you. It was just a scare.

According to the doctors, you are in great health, so there's nothing to worry about."

Amber looked confused. Her mind was hazy, and she could barely remember anything. Slowly, glimpses and flashbacks began to pop up in her mind. She remembered when she was sitting and meditating. She remembered pieces of the journey she had experienced in the privacy of her mind. She remembered seeing Simone, suddenly, she remembered it all.

Her eyes widened, and she quickly sat up on the bed.

"I remember what happened!" she said, looking down to her bed with her hand still placed firmly over her chest. "I need a minute. Would you guys mind?" Amber asked politely for everyone to give her some space as her confusion seem to rise gradually.

They walked out the room, and Amber stood up immediately, feeling completely well. She looked for her journal, and as soon as she found a pen, she began to write:

> Oh, my God. Okay, I remember seeing Master Wolf. I remember walking beside him peacefully in a snow-covered pine tree forest, and I remember him telling me to enter a dark cave. He said I couldn't get out until I was completely healed. It felt so real, I could feel the temperature of the snow-filled scene. I remember a pack of wolves, especially one that was white. One of his eyes was brown, and the other blue. I felt such a powerful magnetic pull to that one.

It was so strong, and it felt like I knew him.
I feel so foggy. I went inside the cave, and I
remember reuniting with Simone ...

Amber stopped writing for a bit and just stared at a
distance, overwhelmed with emotions, memories, and
images coming back into her mind. Her body felt sleepy,
although she had no idea how long she had been asleep.
She didn't remember seeing any doctors, and she didn't
remember the emergency room. She tried to continue
writing in her journal anything she could remember
before it would fade away and be forgotten.

I remember Simone and how...

She paused again in disbelief of her memories. If it
hadn't been for the fact that it felt so real and it had
literally made her pass out, she would have considered
that it may have been just another crazy dream. There
was not even a tiny part of her that thought it was
a dream. She knew everything she remembered had
happened. She felt the energy around it seeming very
light.

Amber lay on her back over the bed, again staring at
the ceiling with her journal still opened over her lap. She
remembered the guidance received about the years to
come. She didn't know how she felt about that. Although
it seemed logical that she would be excited with all this
talk about her big mission and how powerful she was,
the truth was that she didn't know what to do with

that information. She remained in silence, on her bed, wondering and trying to grasp the magnitude of what had just happened.

Victoria opened her bedroom door slightly, peeking to see if it was okay for her to come in. Amber moved back to a sitting position as she waved for her to come in. Victoria sat by the edge of her bed, looking relaxed and serene.

"Hey, how are you feeling?" Victoria asked, handing Amber a cup of black tea she had prepared for her.

"I'm good—a bit confused, but good." Amber held the mug in her hands gratefully.

As usual, Amber got excited to see if there were any messages on the tea label hanging from the tea bag. There was. The message read: "You are healed."

Amber thought that was a freakish coincidence, but her face couldn't hide the mental blur she was experiencing.

"What was that all about? Do you remember anything?" Victoria asked Amber curiously. "Sarah told me she found you passed out while sitting on your meditation pillow. I was wondering if you had experience trouble on another realm or something. I've been worried since yesterday when she told me," Victoria admitted.

Amber shook her head, reassuring her everything was fine. "No, no, on the contrary. I think it is the best thing that has ever happened to me. I'm not quite sure how it all went down, but I know it was a great thing. My mind seems to be putting all of the pieces together." Amber took a sip of the hot black tea and continued to share with Victoria. "This is going to sound so crazy to you ...

well, maybe not. Simone has, somehow, volunteered to continue teaching me through, well, what sounds like the hardest years of my life coming up and I received a heart chakra replacement" Amber tried to wrap her whole experience with the most basic words she could think of.

"What? Is that a thing? Victoria's eyes widened in disbelief of what she had just heard.

"Apparently! I mean, they can do anything, I think. It's just that this is very impressive. In the short time I've been awake, I feel like my heart skips a beat sometimes. It's so bizarre." Amber giggled, realizing how crazy her story was.

"Wow." Victoria spent some time just looking at her. They stared at each other calmly as she added, "It has to be true otherwise why would you wound up in the ER. A regular Higher Self meditation would never get you there, not even a strong one. It sounds to me like, maybe, you've been chosen?"

CHAPTER 39

The chosen ones are those who can bear much pain but cannot bear resentment. Revenge will never be an option to a chosen one. Even in the deepest sense of despair, they would never wish evil onto others consciously. Their sense of honor is permanent, and their ethic is non-negotiable. They are aware, they perceive way more than they admit, and they keep their discoveries close to their hearts.

They pick up on people's intentions, and they see what others don't see. They know what others can't imagine them knowing. They are not pushy; they're serene. They allow others to underestimate them on daily basis to see how far they would go. They observe silently. Their kindness is often mistaken as a weakness, and they can sense it. The purity of their hearts will always surpass their common sense, and they would need to be grounded to function in the society we're living in.

The chosen ones live a lonely existence sometimes,

because they understand the depths of the human ego. They know there's no one to blame, but there are distances that often need to be taken from humanity in general. They are cheerful, happy, and joyful in their personalities, yet sometimes distant in their hearts. They have lived eons, and they can perceive it, even if they don't understand it. They don't fear the complete surrender toward their spiritual paths. They understand that nothing else really exists.

The chosen ones know that the meaningful moments in life are those ordinary moments filled with spontaneity, appreciation, and the kind of gratitude that is felt in the heart. The chosen ones are not afraid to find their life purpose. They have been looking for something; even if they don't understand what it is, they have been looking. They crave that moment when they discover how to fulfil their long-awaited soul's desire. Chosen ones give into their purpose entirely, knowing they are here on Earth just passing by. They understand they have limited time in this incarnation, and they are ready to make the most of it.

The chosen ones don't usually have an easy life; instead, they are pushed to live all forms of difficult scenarios at early ages to develop the capacity to understand, help, and heal others. They are compassionate with everybody, because they can profoundly feel the pain other beings are going through. They are kind, supportive, and genuine, even if no one is looking. Their purity makes them eligible to be chosen.

The Universe has brought these beings to Earth to heal others. Whether it is through their words, their actions, or their professions, they find a way to bring love into this planet. Many chosen ones become obscured by their wounds, ridiculed by their attributes, and they begin to play small to feel safe. Many chosen ones unconsciously choose to become hard, tough, and insensitive, thinking this is the only way to survive this reality.

Many chosen ones begin to believe that their lives are not going to amount to much. They allow their hopes, dreams, and wishes to dim down and even disappear sometimes. No matter how lost they may feel, they will always have a sense of longing for their souls' mysterious desires. Something will always be missing, until it's not. They will be guided into finding their purpose when the time is right, and once they find it, nothing will ever be the same. They will feel attracted to it. Whether it is writing, healing, coaching, traveling, or public speaking, they will feel inspired to transform their current reality completely in order to surrender into this newfound purpose. They will face fears and insecurities toward following their purpose. They may even doubt the validity of their dreams, but as soon as they accept that their dreams and preferences are there for a reason, they will recognize their purpose.

Chosen ones will be the most dedicated students in their pursuits. They will feel hungry for knowledge and spiritual development. They will enjoy being a student, but deep down, they know they are wise teachers and masters. They will give into their education and skills, becoming naturally great at what they do. They will begin to feel inspired, grateful, and fulfilled as soon as they begin to encounter their purpose. Once they are sure about it, they will begin to inevitably move the masses.

The chosen ones are destined for greatness. Regardless of whether they feel comfortable with it at first, they have been chosen for it. They will have massive impact on the world around them, and people will begin to find inspiration in them, in their ways, and in their example. Whatever they do to fulfil their purpose will benefit from word of mouth. One person will share with another, and that way it will become inevitable for the chosen ones to be known. Their success is a given, because their only purpose is to share the light through the gifts and passions they have received.

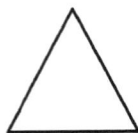

CHAPTER 40

Modern society educates people in such a way that they are expected to blend in with the crowds and fit into a determined mold. When an individual is guided into finding her voice, her power, and her message to share with the world, the individual experiences fear of rejection among many other blocks that can be difficult to perceive and fully understand. People are taught that it's safer to blend in with the crowds than to stand out. They are taught that there's one path to success, and all others are dangerous. Some feel like they are not supposed to take up space in the world being who they are, when that's exactly what they should do.

When people are faced with the possibility of owning a lot of power, it is very common to feel afraid. It is very common to think it's okay for others to have power, but not themselves. What if they use it in the wrong way? What if they are not comfortable being leaders? What if they weren't made for that? These are questions everyone faces when presented with the possibility of stepping up into personal power and claiming their dreams. Everybody in the world has felt not good enough at certain points in life. Everyone feels inadequate sometimes, and everyone feels confused, judged, small, and sad from time to time. The thing is, true leaders are those who act despite these thoughts and feelings, acknowledging they deserve, just like everybody else, to have their messages be heard by the masses. True leaders know they deserve, just like everybody else, to be cherished, honored, and respected. The world is being changed on daily basis by people who have stepped into their power.

A person may ask herself: *Who am I to change the world around me? Who am I to teach others something? Who am I to become powerful?* There is a part of a person that doesn't believe she can, and another part of doesn't believe it's safe. People know they will experience resistance coming from others. The truth is, miracles happen daily, and the happier people are, the happier everything around them becomes. It is worth the struggle. It is the public's responsibility to fulfil the mission; otherwise, they are taking away from all the people out there who are waiting for help.

LAST CHAPTER

Amber rested for a few days before continuing her life as usual. She completely surrendered onto her routine for a few months, focusing on developing her abilities and practicing everything she'd learned. She saw more patients than she thought her body could allow and mastered the principles through trial and error. After a few months had gone by, she began to feel better than ever. Everything was flowing perfectly again until it wasn't. The prophecy received proved to be true and the challenges began.

It was a rainy Sunday morning, and Amber was holding a yellow coffee mug as she sat down on her Moroccan-looking meditation pillow. Her bedroom was colorful and filled with ethnic fabric-covered pillows and throws. Lights adorned the white drapes covering all windows except one, which allowed the views of the city to be seen. She was still sleepy, and the energy of the day felt slow. She wrapped herself in a blanket as she sat down crossed-legged and placed the mug on the floor. She was getting ready to start her morning routine of meditation and gratitude, but as she was about to begin, one of her journals caught her attention from all the way on the other side of her bedroom. The journal's bright-red color seemed to sparkle, inviting her to use it, so she stood up instinctively to reach out for it.

As she sat down, she caressed the red leather cover with her fingers, feeling gratitude in her heart for all the experiences recorded in it. Rain was pouring against her cold bedroom window, and the world still slept. Amber began to feel a deep sense of nostalgia—one that only comes after realizing that all she recorded in there had turned out for the best. It had all turned out right. She had stepped into her own power, more than ever before, in those previous months and even though she knew about the challenges ahead, she was grateful. She had transformed into a secure, mature, and wiser woman. She no longer admired or respected people who didn't deserve this from her. She didn't allow anyone or anything to occupy her valuable mental space. She had become like a solidly grounded tree that couldn't be moved or messed with. She had earned the respect of those around her and above her. She had earned the respect of her spirit guides as well. They had decided to educate her directly, with no need for an intermediary or teacher in physical form. As she allowed her fingers to travel through the sepia pages that held flower petals, dust, and coffee stains, she felt inclined to read what she had written during those months.

Journal Entry 1

April 14, 2015

I feel blessed. This last week something mayor happened. I still can't seem to completely embrace what it means, but I know it is huge. I have been receiving a lot of guidance as far as new ways to do things. At first I was resistant, feeling a little intimidated about messing up. Then, up there, all my guides seemed to start pushing me to get out of my comfort zone by having me make the most ridiculous mistakes. I left the city to go to an important event, and when I was arriving at my destination, which was five hours away by car, I realized I had completely messed up. I had left the crystal back at home with a dense energy I had just removed from a patient inside of it. I freaked out because I remembered, back when I was on the course, that the same thing had happened to one of the students by accident, and she was treated harshly consequently. I considered driving the whole way back and ruining my whole weekend, but something inside me told me it would be all right. I'm always so careful. It had never happened before, and I now understand it happened for a reason.

I was staying in a small wooden cabin in the woods with enough space for myself. As soon as I put down my bags, I began preparing the space for meditation. I was worried, I was nervous, and I felt I would have to face profound consequences. That's where I realized I had been educated to be fearful in my spiritual path. As I sat down and closed my eyes, I saw one of my guides expecting me. He said I didn't need to feel guilty or worried. He had personally manipulated my thoughts for me to forget and face this moment. Step by step, he guided me into cleaning the physical crystal, which was left back at home, only using my mind. We were taught to verify if the crystal was clear or not using a pendulum, which is basically a triangular crystal stone. The pendulum is usually only held by a thin chain, and the way it moves indicates if the crystal is clean. I carefully did everything my guide asked me to do and nervously proceeded to complete each step, in meditation. As soon as I was done, I called Sarah who was back at home with the crystal to verify if the crystal was, indeed, clean. She did, and it was clean. It had been cleaned at a distance, only using my thoughts. That had been one of the best and happiest moments in my spiritual path. Not only I had discovered my mind could alter, move, and transform objects at a distance, but it also meant I would never again have to hide around my parking lot finding a place to create a small bonfire on daily basis. In the shamanic traditions, I have been initiated in, after going ahead with an extraction therapy and removing a negative or destructive energy from a patient, that energy was held inside the extraction crystal. This crystal needed to go through a powerful ceremony that involved fire, prayers, and a whole production to liberate this dense energy and guide it toward where it belongs. After doing more than one therapy a day, it became very annoying to try to fit the ceremony that would clean the crystal into the fast-paced city lifestyle I'm living. It couldn't be done indoors, so I would do it behind my car in my parking lot. It drained my energy trying to remain focused when neighbors would walk near my space, probably wondering what kind of madness I was doing. I did the best I could, but as soon as I realized I could do this with my mind, I felt a huge relief! It also made me understand that even if I had felt that the benefit of having a teacher was temporarily out of reach for me, I was being taught just as clearly, from other realms. What else could be done? Can you imagine?

Amber looked up after reading her own words and smiled gently, feeling warmth toward her innocence at the time when the entry was written. She continued to flip through the pages, which included drawings, lists, and writings about her occasional breakdowns filled with confusion and pain. It was beautiful—all of it. Her practice and way of doing things had developed so rapidly, the memories of those times felt so tender and cute. Everything was different now, she had become agile in the spirit realms which, while writing that entry, she'd never even seen before.

Journal Entry 2

> I still can't believe I can do entire procedures on patients just using my mind. I have learned how to clear, clean, and harmonize patients' chakras with my mind, just needing their consent. I'm impressed we are capable of extracting entities, dense energies, and basically any form of imbalance through thoughts only. Healing therapies are more powerful this way, somehow. They are easier and faster for me too. I feel like a whole world is beginning to open in front of me. I feel like the course has given me great basics, and now my spirit guides are building up on top of that. What a magical feeling it is to know, for the rest of my life, the teachers I have literally live inside of me. I have finally

reached a state of complete gratitude for all that happened with Simone, even if it was painful. Now I understand. If I would have continued only seeking her teachings, I would've never been open enough to receive direct teachings from my spirit guides. I'm so grateful now and realize it just had to go down that way.

Amber laughed, reminiscing how those first-time discoveries felt. It had all felt so new to her back then. Now she had gotten used to the constant guidance and used it to develop her abilities. She moved a strand of her soft brown hair behind her ear as she continued to smile gently. She took a sip of her warm coffee and continued to flip through the pages, amazed by the beauty of these memories. So much had happened up until that point. It seemed like those entries were written years ago, yet only months had gone by.

Journal Entry 3

I was driving back home from the studio last night, and I drove by a car accident. I naturally feel moved by those kinds of things and sent loving energy their way, wishing for everything to turn out for the best. Last night, however, I saw something that was very interesting. In a split-second I saw two projections of me, like holograms ... I'd like to refer to them that way. They were like clones—exact copies of me. They had halos and wings, and they left my body and went directly to the accident.

I continued to drive by naturally, wondering what had just happened and if what I had perceived was accurate. I had no intention to do that. I had no idea I could just send copies of myself to different places. It felt like they just came out of me without my consent, knowing exactly what they needed to do. I continued to drive home. I was thinking about a thousand other things, so I didn't give it that much thought at all. I went home, showered, and did some yoga before bed, and while I was falling asleep, I saw them again. They both popped into my mind. Two identical copies of me, which looked like angels. They had halos and huge white feathery wings that reached the floor. They just stood there, completely uninvited, yet welcomed by me. I immediately woke up from the sleepy state I was in and observed them carefully in my mind.

"You can do this however many times you need. From this moment on, you can be in all places at all times. Your higher self will control and guide each one of us— versions of you. You can send yourself to all world crises, big accidents, or any form

215

of misfortune, all at once, and you will be helping and assisting others without your energy diminishing in any way."

Wait. What? As I write this, I can barely believe it. Dreams come true. Dreams you never thought possible can come true.

After this journal entry Amber's green eyes began to look around her bedroom, acknowledging how different life was at that point and reminding herself of the magnitude of that, which had become normal to her. It is easy to get used to things, even the things that represent major breakthroughs in life and history. For her, this was normal now. She wondered how something so miraculous could become normal. How could she go about her life, knowing she had become capable of doing things few humans even consider possible?

She took a few minutes to reminisce and to begin feeling the magic of what that first leap of faith transformed her life into. She remembered all the rituals and all the moments when she experienced fear. She also remembered the different tests the Universe put them all through. She remembered the first time she realized she could "see" things in her mind. This memory brought tenderness and innocence into her heart. She remembered how life felt before all this magic had entered her life. She remembered what her life was like before shamanism.

Gratitude infused the air, and she decided to put the journal away. Amber took a few minutes to breathe and thank the Universe for all the beautiful experiences contained in the previous years of her life. She closed her eyes. Her eyelids felt heavy, and she allowed herself to indulge in the memories. They appeared in her mind, one after the other. As she observed all the details, she did so slowly and peacefully. She took the time to honor each memory that made her path look the way it did now. She delighted herself in the emotions surfacing, and a tear dropped rapidly down her chin. As she danced with her past in unbelievable pleasure, she began to feel inspired by the future ahead.

As she opened her eyes again, a few minutes of enjoyment later, she saw Master Wolf, her spirit guide, waiting for her. He sat peacefully in front of her meditation spot, manifested into physical form. He didn't surprise her that much anymore, but after reliving those memories, she couldn't help seeing him with renewed eyes. Silently, they stared at each other, savoring the encounter before any one of them would speak.

As they remained in silence, only the distant sound of the rain was present. The bedroom was darkened by the cloudy sky outside, and only peace remained. Master Wolf began to lean closer to Amber, and holding eye contact, he whispered, "It has come the time for you to teach."

The End

GLOSSARY

Andean lineage: A linear descent from an ancestor, in this case referring to the mighty civilization that inhabited the Andes mountain range region. Neo shamans of today's world are considered to have evolved from earlier Andean predecessors, maintaining the lineage alive nowadays.

Animal spirit/totem: According to ancient traditions, a totem is a spirit being, sacred object, or symbol of a tribe, clan, family, or individual. These spirit beings in the form of animals act as guides in the person's life, providing archetypical and symbolic teachings that connect the person to the spirit world.

Archetypical spirit: Visual symbol or energetic imprint manifested through a guiding spirit. Designed to trigger your memory of why you are here and the truth behind the illusion of reality. These archetypical spirits can often convey messages that verbal and written information cannot.

Ayni: In Quechua language, the concept of reciprocity or mutualism, practiced among people of the Andean mountain communities.

Chakras: Each of the centers of spiritual power inside the human range, believed to be part of the subtle body, not the physical body. The direct translation from Sanskrit is the word *wheel*, resembling a wheel of energy flow that enables our spiritual experience in this physical world.

Earthbound spirit: A human spirit that has not properly passed over into the next world, or heaven. Therefore, it remains bound to the physical realm.

Entity / fluid energy: A conscious energy form inhabiting or embodying a being, place, object, or natural phenomenon. Also understood as nonphysical energy parasites with a consciousness of its own that attach to a person's subtle energy body, similar to the way a physical parasite does.

Higher self: An eternal, omnipotent, conscious, and intelligent being that represents one's real self beyond our linear, ego-bound identities.

Homo luminous being: A next evolutionary level for humanity, proposed by various prophecies across indigenous cultures, particularly the medicine tradition of the Inca. For the Inca shaman, it consists on a quantum leap made by humankind at the dawn of the twenty-first century, which is meant to bring peace, truth, light, and harmony for a new era of consciousness on Earth.

Kuyas: Sacred stones that serve as a spiritual guidance in shamanic healing ceremonies. These provide diagnostic information about a patient, as well as particular teachings to be drawn out during a healing ceremony.

Law of attraction: The attractive, magnetic power of the Universe that draws similar energies together. It manifests through the power of creation, everywhere and in many ways and forms. This law attracts thoughts, ideas, people, situations, and circumstances, eventually taking us to the realization that since we essentially manifest what we attract, we are therefore the masters of our own universe.

Mandala: In ancient Hindu and Buddhist symbolism, a geometric figure representing the universe and its different layers of manifestation. Often referred to as a circle of life, mandalas offer balancing visual elements, symbolizing the unifying harmonies of the universe.

Munay-Ki rites: A series of nine empowerment rites based on the initiatory practices of the Q'ero shamans of Peru, as taught by anthropologist Alberto Villoldo. *Munay* in Quechua means "love and will," together with *ki*, from the Japanese word for energy, combine to give the meaning: energy of love.

Pendulum: A tool used to communicate with spirit via the assistance of higher selves and spiritual guides. In spiritual tradition, they are regarded as an effective instrument that can help the practitioner to confidently carry out diagnosis about a specific case.

Pi stone: Pi stones date back to the Incas and are symbolic of our luminous bodies and the energetic universe. They are used as star gates and energy keys, making them powerful tools for learning, healing, and ritual initiations.

Playing small: Essentially, the act of holding your gifts, talents, and spiritual light repressed within yourself rather than sharing them with the world and expanding it throughout the Universe. It manifests in the human experience through insecurity, low self-esteem, anxiety, doubt, fear, loneliness, and others.

Psychic: Having a special mental and intuitive ability; a heightened sensibility that goes beyond senses and that can either enable the person to predict or see events/things that haven't still manifested in the physical world.

Sacred geometry: Known as the fundamental building blocks of our Universe, based on mathematics and form. Sacred geometry can be found in all of nature in golden mean proportions, Fibonacci spirals, hexagonal structures, pentagonal structures, platonic solid structures, crystal structures, tube torus, etc.

Sacred space: A place of veneration and communion with the spirit world, achieved through a specific ritual and taking the form of healing sphere that is pure, holy, and safe. A sacred space is a place for summoning the healing power of nature, removing our pain and fear derived on the notion that Earth is not a safe place.

Self-mastery: The ability to take control of one's life without being blown off course by feelings, urges, or external circumstances. Achieved through practice, discipline, and energy management and understanding.

Shadow: An unconscious aspect of a person's personality, which the conscious ego does not identify in itself. In the words of psychotherapist Carl Jung, the shadow is the unknown dark side of a person's personality.

Shamanic journey: Known as the most common of spiritual traditions that a shaman performs, with the help of rhythmic percussion or sound and involving the interaction with spirits such as power animals, spiritual teachers, and angels. Through this close contact, a shaman receives life guidance and instruction for further understanding of life situations.

Shamanic sacred fire ceremony: A shamanic technique for purification involving the primary element of fire, in which the practitioner sets an intention of release, renewal, and healing.

Shamanism: A practice found among various ancient cultures that consists in reaching altered states of consciousness to perceive and interact with a spirit world and channel these transcendental energies into this world.

Soul: The spiritual or immaterial part of a living being. In shamanism, the soul is known as the axis mundi, the center of the healing arts, which can travel beyond our bodies to achieve specific healing purposes.

Star Keeper's Rite: One of the nine Munay-Ki rites of the Q'ero shamans in Peru. This rite prepares the practitioner for the time to come and sets up our luminous body to shine with the light of the sun, expanding the person's being to places throughout time, out to the stars, and beyond. Upon receiving this rite, the physical body begins to evolve into the Homo luminous body.

Stone people: Spiritual attributions to apparently inanimate objects. In Shamanic traditions, everything possesses its own spirit. Some stones have a higher spiritual value, providing wisdom, love, and medicine to the shaman and his or her patients.

Vibrational frequency: The rate at which the atoms and sub-particles of a specific being or object vibrate. It is believed that the higher this vibrational frequency is, the closer it is to the frequency of light. Under this belief, each word we speak and thought we think sends out a vibration that attracts to it an experience of like vibration. If we send out fear, we attract fear. If we send out love, we attract love.

Wisdom Keeper's Rite: Another important Munay-Ki rite, which connects the person to a lineage of luminous beings from the past and future. It offers the gifts of the divine masculine, connecting the practitioner to this energy and completing the balance with the energy obtained from the Day Keeper's Rite.

EPILOGUE

(Conclusion of the Book)

There are deeper truths to our day-to-day lives, and we have the option of seeing past the illusion to receive those insights. Every person who has presented us challenges, difficulties, and problems has a deeper agenda—a beautiful one. Those who we consider enemies, rivals, or toxic characters in our lives have all sacrificed themselves to teach us these lessons out of pure love. We came to this Earth with a plan, and we are all in this together. All competition is an illusion. All deception and trouble are illusions of this earthly plane. The best teachers and the ones we must be grateful of are those who have put their own self-image aside, consciously or unconsciously, to continue teaching us.

Always follow your heart. You know better than any human around you. You are being guided always. Allow yourself to be guided. Avoid giving your power to other people or circumstances. You truly know best.

For more information about the author, visit WWW.AWAKENEDWILDCHILD.COM or follow her on IG: @awakenedwildchild8 / FB: Awakened Wild Child

READER'S GUIDE

This book can also be enjoyed in book clubs or reading gatherings. It is recommended for groups of –eight to sixteen participants, all willing to share their own experiences openly. After reading the whole book, it would be ideal for all participants to allow the information to sink in gradually. See how it feels for them after a few days. Then, while gathered in a group, discuss the following questions openly:

1. Do you agree or disagree with the idea of a seemingly invisible world of spirits permanently coexisting with our physical world?
2. Do you agree or disagree that the most challenging characters in our lives intend to help us evolve and grow at a soul level?
3. Do you agree or disagree with the existence of high vibrations and low vibrations?
4. Do you agree or disagree with the existence of apparitions, ghosts, and dark spirits?
5. Do you believe in angels, spirit guides, and ascended masters?
6. Have you ever tried to connect with them? If so, share with the group the best ways you like to connect.

7. What is your biggest takeaway, quote, or lesson from this book?

To use this book for personal healing:

1. Grab a journal.
2. Prepare yourself some coffee or tea.
3. Snuggle up in your favorite spot.
4. Call upon your angels and ask them to help you heal through these contemplations.
5. Ask yourself the following questions:
   a. How would you define God based on your own personal experiences and perspectives, being completely honest to yourself?
   b. In your life now, what makes you feel expansive and happy? What makes you feel constricted and small?
   c. If you could do anything with your life (no limits), what would you choose for yourself?
   d. List the ten most painful moments or situations you have lived in your life.
   e. Allow yourself to write openly about these ten situations, pouring out all your most hidden feelings and wounds. Honor the pain. It's there for a reason.
   f. Burn the papers lovingly with the intention to have these energies released from your system for your highest good and healing.
   g. Thank your angels and spirit guides, and consider yourself healed. Repeat out loud: "I am healed. I let it be so, and so it is."

.

Manufactured by Amazon.ca
Bolton, ON